I0772728

never rest

MARSHALL THORNTON

KENMORE BOOKS

Published by Kenmore Books

Edited by Jerry Wheeler

Cover design by Marshall Thornton

Images by 123rf stock

ISBN: 979-8-9902397-6-0

Hardcover edition.

✿ Created with Vellum

acknowledgments

For their ongoing support and friendship, I would like to thank Jeanie Williams, Jennie Evenson, Randy and Valerie Trumbull, Roberta Degnore, Danielle Wolff, Jerry Wheeler, Nathan Bay, Catherine McCabe, and Joan Martinelli.

one

I was ready. It was time to go. I was embarking on a journey to the great beyond; I was passing over; biting the big one; crossing rainbow bridge; meeting my maker; kicking the bucket; cashing in my chips; pushing up daisies or some other trivial euphemism for the thing that could not be spoken. I'd packed my emotional baggage and was set. All I needed to do was say a few goodbyes—preferably without using any euphemisms or even the word goodbye—and that was that. Well, except for the waiting. Though, I was pretty sure there wouldn't be much more of that. Finally.

Almost five years ago, right before I turned fifteen, people stopped asking what I wanted to be when I grew up because it was obvious I wasn't going to. That's when I got my diagnosis. Acute blah-blah-blah leukemia. That's what I heard, anyway. The words that doctors use in those situations have way too many syllables making them almost impossible to remember. I think that's a marketing tool. Like, if you can't really remember what it is you're sick with you have to go back to the doctor and pay them to tell you again. Not that my mom didn't call back that same afternoon and hound the secretary until she got the right name and spelling so she could Google the crap out of acute blah-blah-blah leukemia.

A battle. People like to call it a battle. I battled cancer for nearly five years. The battle went something like this: chemo, chemo, chemo, recovery from chemo, disappointing results, chemo, chemo, more recovery, unofficial remission, nosebleeds, dizzy spells, anemia, remission denied, clinical trial, chemo, chemo, chemo, a slowing of the disease process, chemo, chemo, a speeding up of the disease process, chemo, chemo, chemo, trying to get well enough to have more chemo and who knows what's next. Well, I know what's next. Surrender. The battle ends.

It's a lame battle if you think about it. One that takes place while sitting in waiting rooms reading magazines, in comfy reclining chairs with hanging bags of clear toxic fluids slowly dripping into you, bouts of vomiting, endless days of reality TV—the marathon days are my favorites—hair loss, weight loss, edema, weight gain, books started but not finished, bruises where the nurse hunted for veins that refused to be found, bruises where nothing happened at all, college classes attempted and withdrawn from, parental tears hidden in the night. No, if it was really a battle, I would have gotten to punch someone. And I would have liked to punch someone. At least at the start.

"We're going to fight this," was the first thing my mother said on diagnosis day. We sat, a little stunned—maybe a lot stunned—in her super-mom-ish Toyota Rav-4 on the fourth floor of a parking garage that seemed to be made completely of concrete, soot, and chewed bubble gum. I wanted to accuse her of being unoriginal. I mean the line was straight off basic cable. But what was she going to say?

"You know what? Let's give up. Why don't I cash in my 401K, and we'll go to Vegas and spend the money gambling and drinking and hiring escorts."

Actually, that would have been a lot more fun than the way things went.

I'm telling this completely bass-ackwards. Let me start again. My name is Jake Margate. Jake is not short for Jacob or any other name. It's my actual name. Don't ask me why. I live with my mom right outside of Chicago in Niles, Illinois. I'm almost twenty. I've had acute blah-blah-blah leukemia for nearly five years.

Wait, I said that already. Shit.

Anyway, the doctors are super proud of themselves that I've lived this long. My blast cells were through the roof when I was diagnosed, and the end of my road was supposed to happen almost two years ago. Every extra day I spend binge-watching *America's Top Model* is a victory for my doctors.

You see, they, too, are battling cancer. They charge in, the good guys in white coats, discussing the merits of this poison or that poison, and then they fill me up with whichever one is most touted in some obscure medical journal which may or may not have been paid by the maker of said nasty poison to tout said nasty poison. They ask how I am but never hear anything more than how my symptoms have changed. Which ones are new? Which ones are side effects from the treatment? Which ones have left or returned or never gone away? They prescribe something new and then charge out of the room.

Honestly, I don't feel like I'm battling cancer. But I do feel like a battlefield.

At the end of my last doctor's visit, they didn't prescribe anything but morphine. A lot of morphine. They asked to see me alone. I'm an adult now, after all, and I don't need my mommy there to hold my hand. Totally in character, my mom refused to leave the room. So they asked *me* to leave.

It might have been amusing if I hadn't figured out what they were saying to her. They were telling her I was going to die soon, and she needed to prepare me. She needed to prepare herself. I guessed that the plan was to give her a wake-up call and then have me come back in to speak to them alone. But that isn't the way it worked out. After a few minutes, my mother stormed out of the office and announced we were leaving.

"Um, I think they wanted to tell me something."

"They're not telling you anything. I fired them."

"But. They're *my* doctors. Shouldn't I decide—"

"It's my insurance. I pay the co-pays. I fired them."

I was nauseated. And by that, I mean nauseated in a completely different way than the way chemo nauseates you. This was emotional nausea. Pure puke-inducing emotion. Something was going terribly wrong, and I didn't know how to stop it.

I've wandered off again, haven't I? I'm not sure if that's a symptom or a side effect. I'm hoping it's one or the other. I'd hate for it to be my personality. Okay, what was I was saying?

My dad. My dad lives in Park Ridge with his new wife. Park Ridge is one suburb and two or three income levels away from Niles. My mother hates him and, though she would never ask it, wants me to hate him, too.

The way she acts, you'd think he cheated on her with Amelia—that's my stepmom—but he didn't. They didn't even meet until my parents had been divorced for a year. No, for my mom, it was a much bigger betrayal. He became a success.

When she married my father, he was a struggling musician who supported himself doing temporary office work and random computer stuff. In fact, they met in the bank where my mother was an executive assistant—where she's still an executive assistant. Some of this has always been a little fuzzy, but I think they dated a little, she got pregnant, and they decided to do the right thing and get married. Even when I was a little kid, I could see that doing the right thing was often completely the wrong thing.

My mom wanted my dad to make something of himself, in particular something that had a decent income attached. She's not the greedy sort, though. She's the nervous sort and has the idea that money makes you safe. Unfortunately, my dad steadfastly refused to do anything of the kind. According to her, every good thing that happened to them when they were married was my mother's doing, and it's true she organized our moving out of a one-bedroom apartment in Roger's Park and into a small brick two-bedroom house with a collapsing garage on an eighth of an acre in Niles.

Occasionally unemployed and still trying to get weekend gigs at Chicago pubs, my father was less and less the man of my mother's dreams. She finally threw him out when I was around eight. I have no idea what the last straw was. He probably lost a job or quit a job or decided to go to Milwaukee for a few weeks with his band to play some gigs. I don't know. And as much as my mom likes to rant about what a loser my dad used to be, she leaves out a lot of specifics.

After she threw him out, as though to spite her, my dad promptly invented some bit of software that helped lawyers track their billing down to the quarter-cent. Money began to roll in like a tidal wave, and very soon he acquired my stepmom, her two little kids, and a five thousand square foot home in Park Ridge where I spent my weekends roaming around trying to avoid my steplings. When I was thirteen, my dad and Amelia had a set of twins all their own: fraternal, boy and girl. I thought the whole *Yours, Mine and Ours* thing was kind of a drag, and I managed to find excuses not to see them for a while. My dad seemed not to mind much—

he *was* busy, after all—but then I got acute blah-blah-blah leukemia, and he wanted me to call him every day. Something I never got good at.

My iPhone rang and a semi-embarrassing picture of my dad playing a gig with his band of semi-pathetic middle-aged dudes popped up. I put *Project Runway All Stars* on mute and accepted the call.

"Hey buddy," he said.

"Hey."

"How's today?" People had started to avoid asking me how I felt too directly.

"Shitty." My usual answer was "better than yesterday" but there are only so many years you can tell that lie.

"Yeah. Listen, I've been thinking about something. You know the money I put aside for your college?"

He'd been nice enough to sock some money away for me in a college fund. But I'd barely touched it. I'd tried a couple of cheap classes at Oakton but couldn't show up often enough to figure out what they were about. I did better with an online course I took but, seriously, what was the point?

"Yeah?"

"Maybe you should use that money for anything you want."

"Oh, yeah. Thanks." I was ready. I'd stopped wanting things. And I was pretty sure they didn't let you bring money where I was going.

"So, what do you think you want? Do you want to buy something? How about a computer? Yours is ancient. Or a new car?" He'd already given me Amelia's old Sedona van which I never drove anyway and not just because it was a totally humiliating vehicle. I mean a minivan was the worst, but I would have been happy to be humbled if I'd had the energy to turn the steering wheel.

He left a long pause. I knew he wanted to play a private, father-son episode of Make-A-Wish, but I seriously wasn't up to it. I knew what I wanted, and I knew he couldn't help me with it. Or could he?

"Look Dad, there is something you could do for me."

"What's that?"

"Get Mom to let go."

"Let go? Of you?"

"Yeah. It's time."

He was silent for a really long time.

"Oh Jake, I don't know. Your mom never lets go of anything. And this is a pretty tall order. You mean the world to her."

"Can you try?"

"Are you sure it's time? Maybe you're just feeling a little down. That would be understandable. You've been through—"

"I'm the only one who's going to know when it's time, Dad. And it's time."

For a little bit, I didn't know if he was going to say anything at all. "All right. If that's what you want," he said with all the enthusiasm of the condemned. "You mean the world to me, too. I didn't mean to make it sound—"

"It's okay. I get it."

He had spares. My mom didn't. We all knew my dying—I mean, my imminent departure—sucked most for my mom. But that didn't mean it didn't suck for my dad. It just meant it sucked for him with a houseful of kids. And that seemed easier than the way it was going to suck for my mom with an empty house. A spare bedroom was no consolation for losing a son.

I said goodbye to my dad and clicked off. I'd just asked him to help my mom understand that it was going to be soon. A lot of people would have bawled their eyes out for a good hour or two. I just unmuted the TV and fell asleep. I mean, it wasn't like anything really important had just happened. It wasn't like I'd lost a cooking competition or been booted off an island. So, really, I couldn't see the point of crying. I was going to die.

There, I said it. I was going to die which made me exactly like everyone else in the world. There was just one difference: I was ready.

two

If you think I was depressed or sad or even unhappy, you're wrong. If anything, I was relieved. Dying of a terminal illness is like a trip to Detroit. You hear all these terrible things, and you really don't want to go, but when you get there, it's not as bad as you thought it would be. And, if you're thinking my plan was to off myself, you'd be wrong. I didn't want to be spoon-fed a concoction of applesauce and morphine, leaving my mom to face the ire of some heartless prosecutor. All I wanted to do was give up and let it happen. I was ready for nature to take its course. A one-hundred percent certified organic death. That's all I wanted.

My mother, however, had other ideas. She got home at her regular time, which was about three episodes from the end of that day's *Project Runway All Stars* marathon. I wasn't sure who I wanted to win. The girl with the tattoos was probably the most talented, at least at making clothes on a deadline, but the guy with the flat black hair and the disks in his ears—

"I have really good news," my mother said when she walked into my room. I muted the TV that sat on a set of shelves at the foot of my bed, which was a hospital bed my mom got second or third or fourth hand. The mattress was lumpy, but it adjusted so I could semi-sit or lay down, whichever I felt like. The other things in my room were a desk I never sat at; a bureau crammed with clothes I'd worn in junior high school; and a hamper where we put my sheets after I sweat through them at night. The room was still painted dark blue with yellow stars on the ceiling. We'd painted it that way when I was about eleven. I hated it by the time I was thirteen but didn't want to tell that to my mom. I was working my way up to asking if we could repaint about the time I got my diagnosis. Other things seemed more important after that.

"Did Dad call you?" I asked, hoping the good news had something to do with what he was supposed to talk to her about but also not expecting it would.

"Yes. Well, no. He left a message. I know exactly what he wants to talk to me about so I'm not calling him back."

"You do? You know?"

"He said he had something important to tell me about you. That can only mean one thing. Really, Jake, I'm a little offended you couldn't tell me yourself. And why you'd tell your father before you told me—"

"What do you think I'm going to tell you?"

"You know I'll love you no matter what."

Oh my God. I've screwed this up again, haven't I? I need to stop and explain. I'd never actually come out to my mom. I knew I was gay, and she knew I was gay but we didn't talk about it because I wouldn't. Absolutely refused. Every time she hinted or teased or even posed a direct question, I shut her down. And maybe that was mean, but I was jealous. You see, as soon as I got cancer there was another boy on the scene. A boy I call Other Jake.

He was the Jake who never got cancer, or worse, the boy who beat cancer. He was the Jake who instead of laying around the house being chemo sick for weeks on end was out and proud at fifteen. Other Jake told his mom and dad he was gay and, well, anyone else who'd stand still for more than thirty seconds. Other Jake joined the Gay/Straight Alliance at school and was almost immediately elected president. Other Jake fought with the principal over a T-shirt he wore to school that said "You can't pray the gay away." Other Jake went to prom with the nicest boy who was tall with dark hair and gorgeous dark eyes. Other Jake was wicked smart and read classic books even when teachers didn't assign them. Other Jake was going to a good college and planned to major in Queer Studies or maybe Political Science. Most of all, Other Jake was healthy.

And my mom adored him. Honestly, I think I had a little crush on him too. But I knew early on that Other Jake wasn't ever going to be real. So I didn't come out to my mom because it felt like I might be leading her on, teasing her with something that couldn't be, encouraging her to love Other Jake when she really shouldn't.

"Mom—"

"Don't make me be the one to say it. This is *your* moment, Jake. *You* need to say it." She pulled the chair from my desk over to the bed and looked at me intently. When I didn't say anything, she went on. "Everything is going to be okay. Nothing's going to change."

"This isn't what I wanted Dad to talk to you about."

"This what, dear? Go ahead. You can say it. You're..."

"You think I'm coming out? That's what you think, isn't it?"

Maybe it was time. Maybe I should just tell her. If I was dying soon there wasn't any harm in telling her the truth, was there? But then we might never talk about what I really wanted to talk—

"Yes. You're coming out. Finally. I've known for years. I hope that's not offensive. Not being surprised. What did your father say? I'm sure he was clueless. You and I have always had a much stronger bond."

"I didn't come out to Dad."

"You didn't? Then why did he call me and leave that message?"

"Look Mom, I've been sick for a really long time. I mean, yes, I'm gay but that's not what's important."

"Of course, it's important! How can you say it's not important? It's the most important thing in the world."

"Mom, it's not. There was something else I wanted you to talk about with Dad."

"Something else? I don't understand. You're being very strange."

"It's time." My mouth went dry when I said it.

"It's time for what?"

"It's time for you to let go. It's time for me to die."

She burst out laughing. I wondered if she'd completely gone over the edge. I really hoped she hadn't. Giving my mother a nervous breakdown and dying in the same week would really suck.

"Jake, I said I have good news. And I do have good news. I have *wonderful* news. You've been accepted into a new clinical trial just starting up."

"I don't want to do it."

"I haven't even told you about it."

"I don't care. I've been through enough."

"You always do this. You have to trust me, Jake. I've gotten you this far. We need to keep going. We need to keep fighting."

I wanted to tell her she wasn't fighting at all. *I* was the one fighting. Except even that wasn't true. I wasn't fighting. I was just taking a lot of shitty medicines and hoping they didn't kill me before the cancer did. And now she wanted me to take more shitty medicine that would make me feel sicker, which in itself would be an accomplishment because I really didn't know how I could feel sicker.

"No," I said softly.

"The research institute is in Michigan. We leave in the morning."

three

I suppose I should have put up more of a fight, chained myself to the bed or, at the very least, dug my fingernails into the doorjamb and clung for dear life when my mom came to get me. But I'd known her long enough to know when she decided something was going to happen, she made sure it did. Fighting her would only make a miserable situation miserabler. I know that's not a word, but I like it. Miserabler. I woke up miserabler. It sounded like you had marbles in your mouth when you said it. The English language needs more words like that.

Anyway, sorry. Wandered off track again.

The trip to Michigan was supposed to take less than seven hours, but it took more than twelve because I had a seizure outside of someplace called Big Rapids. I'd had a headache pretty much the whole time since we left Cook County. Maybe I should have told my mom to stop and give me something. Maybe it would have warded off the seizure. Or, maybe it wouldn't have.

I'd been haunting WebMD on and off for years—my mom wasn't the only one who Googled. Seizures are a symptom of acute blah-blah-blah leukemia. They are also a side effect of half the chemo I'd had. Plus I'd had seizures before, so it shouldn't have been a surprise.

Well, the ones I had before weren't like this. The ones I'd had before were your basic lost-in-a-daydream kind of seizure which might not even be noticed if they didn't sometimes happen mid-sentence. This one was big. This one was the kind where you get stiff as a board and can't move but can't stop moving either. It's like whatever you want your body to do —being still and sitting in the passenger seat like a normal person—it just won't do. Suddenly, it has got a mind of its own, and the front seat of the car turns into a mosh pit.

Slam dancing while on a long-distance drive is embarrassing but nowhere near as embarrassing as pissing your pants while you're at it. That's what took most of the extra time: finding a place where I could change my clothes and my mom could try to figure out the best way to save the piss-soaked seat in her Rav-4.

We found a Biggby Coffee by some University I'd never heard of and spent a lot of time going back and forth between the car and the rest room. I tried to feel bad about the car, but I had a little trouble. It was only two years old, so I kind of figured it was my mom's own fault. I mean, she bought a new one every three years. When she got this one, she already had a kid with leukemia who was likely to piss or shit or puke or bleed at a moment's notice. You'd think she would have figured out that saving a few bucks and not getting the washable leatherette seats was just a bad idea. I did manage not to tell her that.

I changed my clothes in the men's room while my mother snuck a roll of toilet paper past the barista and went to work on the seat. I was groggy and only marginally aware of what had happened. The seizure made me feel kind of stoned. I'd managed to do my share of crappy weed when I was thirteen and fourteen, in case you're wondering, and I felt like my mother had slipped me a roofie somewhere along the way. In my stoned way, I spent half the time I was putting on my clean pants trying to figure out why my mom would roofie me. I was too out of it to realize that taking me someplace I didn't want to go was actually an excellent reason to drug me.

I tried washing my face, and it turned into a freak-fest because there was this complete stranger in the mirror. I mean, I guess it was me but not a *me* I recognized. And it definitely wasn't Other Jake. No, this guy was like the opposite of Other Jake. This guy was wearing the knit cap I'd put on that morning. The same funky mottled blue one my grandmother had sent me from New Jersey. My mother's mother who we never saw partly because she lived so far away and partly because of some teenage trauma that sort of wrecked their relationship, and no one ever told me about. I always wanted to know what that was about.

Oh shit, I'm off the rails again, aren't I? Sorry.

Back to the can at Biggby Coffee where I was looking into the mirror. The guy I saw there was gaunt and gray and needed a shave and looked more like a hundred and nineteen than nineteen. His mouth kind of hung open, and he looked unhappy and tired. Really tired. Looking at him made me angry with my mom because the person in the mirror, the *me* in the mirror, was going to die. No doubt about it. She'd been looking at *him* a lot longer than I had. How could she not see it? How could she pretend this wasn't happening?

When I got back to the car, she'd put two bath towels on the seat so I could sit down and not get myself wet all over again. The fact that she'd had the forethought to bring a couple of bath towels with her was even more humiliating than pissing on the front seat.

As we pulled back out onto the highway, I said, "I should be in hospice."

"People go to hospice to die."

"No shit."

She ignored that and began to talk about our destination. We were going to The Godwin Institute. "They have an amazing reputation. They're doing cutting edge work."

I was dubious. In five years of having leukemia, I'd never heard anyone mention the place. And it was in Michigan. Nowhere, Michigan. Medical research happened in San Francisco or Chicago or Washington DC or just about anywhere except Nowhere, Michigan.

"Where did you hear about this place?" I asked, not bothering to keep the suspicion out of my voice.

"It was in a chat room."

"A chat room? They still have those?"

"Of course they still have those. I think. I mean, it seemed like a chat room. I may be using the wrong terminology."

"It was probably an app."

"See, a hipster like you knows how to explain things to an oldster like me."

It was weird when my mom called herself old. She'd been just a couple years older than me when I was born. So she was barely forty. It was tough to think about her being my age, though. She was like twenty-two or three and she had a baby. I was nineteen, and all I had was an impending death. Oh God. Maudlin much? I know, I know, feeling sorry myself is unattractive but hey, if not now, when?

Wow, I'm doing it again. Leaving shit out.

Okay, here's the deal with my mom. Cheryl Rogers-Margate is a small woman. Five two. She'd have to finish off an entire chocolate cream pie if she wanted to hit the scale at a hundred pounds. And she's pretty. And tough. And doesn't even look thirty-five, which is considered a big plus when you're over forty.

She should have married again. It should have been easy for her to snag some rich guy except, well, she's got that Napoleonic thing. They say it about men, Napoleon-complex. You know when guys get real aggressive just to make up for the fact that they're short. FYI: Napoleon was this crazy dictator guy who conquered Europe to make up for being height-challenged. See, home-schooling doesn't completely suck. Anyway, don't let anyone tell you it's just men with this Napoleonic issue. My mom had it bad.

"So we're going to this place based on what someone told you in a not-exactly-a-chat room?" This thought flashed, *Abandon hope all ye who enter chat rooms*. God, she would have exploded if I'd said that.

"Take the judgment out of your voice, Jake. I'm not going to talk to you if you're going to be like that."

At that particular moment, I didn't know how else to be, so I shut up. I didn't do much but look out the window for forty miles or so. We were on a narrow two-lane highway going north. Everything I could see was green. Trees seemed to rush the highway and then recede. I could feel them, waiting, hoping for humanity to fall on its collective face so they could grow wherever they damn well pleased. Every movie about the apocalypse is gray and dead, but I don't think the end will be like that. I think the apocalypse will be green. Fertile. Fecund. The revenge of the plants.

I'd calmed down enough that I could say, "So, tell me about this place."

"It's called The Godwin Institute, which I think I said. And yes, I heard about it in on the Internet, but I'm not an idiot. I've researched it, and I've been emailing with the doctor there about your case. Dr. Harry.

He's absolutely brilliant. He's been researching for decades and is up on the latest—"

"Hairy? His name is Hairy?" This was getting worse by the minute.

"No. Harry."

"You mean like Tom, Dick and... that Harry?"

"It's his last name."

"What's his first name, Harold?"

"You're making jokes. That means you feel better."

The grogginess had worn off, and the headache had dialed down. Still. "I feel like I'm dying. If there's a better version of that, I guess I feel it."

As though I said something else entirely, she said, "Good. I'm glad you feel better. I sent Dr. Harry your records."

"How many trips to the post office did that take?"

It was a semi-serious question. I've seen my file. Well, files. After about three inches, they start you a new one. Still, my joke earned a frown from my mom. "I sent the records digitally. Now who's living in the dark ages?"

She was very proud whenever she one-upped me about the latest technology. She loved when she knew things I didn't. Which wasn't exactly fair since I'd been stuck in bed for the last few years while she had an entire IT department to teach her shit.

"I've told Dr. Harry all about you. He can't wait to meet you."

"So this is social? We're just going for tea?"

"Go ahead, make jokes. You don't have to take this seriously. I'll take it seriously for you."

For a minute, I wanted to scream. This was not the first time she'd shouldered the burden of a dying son all on her own.

"Do they specialize in cancer?" I asked, a bit sheepish.

"Mostly."

I had no idea what she meant by mostly. If she was another kid my guess would be that meant, *No, but I don't really want to tell you that*. She was an adult, though, so it might mean that, or it might actually mean mostly. I could have questioned her more. Tried to get to the bottom of it, but I was fading. I was that kind of sick tired where you don't just want to lie down, you want to sink into a bed and let your body spread until it's doing a Salvador Dali thing over the edges.

"I'm going to put the seat back and close my eyes."

I got the seat back and tried to roll over as best I could while wearing a seatbelt and sitting on two fluffy towels. Just as I was letting the exhaustion grab hold of me and pull me into sleep, my mother began to sing "I Will Always Love You." That was her idea of a lullaby, which probably explained more things than I had the energy to think about. The song had been a hit back when she was a kid, I guess, and she used to put me to sleep with it. Her singing it to me now was sweet and creepy and really, really off key.

four

Comfy. I was at home and cozy in my own bed. It felt luxurious, silky, and warm. But then I began to float off it, to float away. I knew I would miss my cozy bed, but it didn't matter. Wherever I was going was comfy, too. I'd be happy there with all of this behind me. I floated up around the stupid yellow stars I'd come to hate. Wanting to get away from them, I looked over at the window. That's where I wanted to be, and then I was, slipping out my bedroom window. Pouring out the window as though I were soup. A soupy kind of a person.

It was night. The moon-bright neighborhood was still, sleeping. I walked down the street, my feet on the ground now, toward the end with the cul-de-sac. Why was I walking down there? It was a dead end. There was nowhere to turn. Then the front door of one of the houses opened. I think it was a family named Meyer who lived there. But it wasn't one of them who came out onto the stoop. Instead, it was a tall, thin man wearing a black, hooded robe and carrying a sickle.

The grim reaper. I giggled. It was ridiculous. I'd seen this character all over the place: in ancient Woody Allen movies, in memes, on greeting cards, hell, whole TV shows starred the grim reaper. I knew he wasn't real. Couldn't be. I laughed again. Then laughed some more. The reaper began to ring like a cellphone. He opened his mouth and out came the melodic little tune. It struck me as hysterically funny. I woke in the middle of a "HA!"

"You're laughing," my mother said. "That's a good sign."

"I had a really lame dream."

"It doesn't matter why you're laughing, Jake. It just matters that you laugh." Laughter was the best medicine. One of my mother's mantras.

The melodic tune that told me I had a text played, and I pulled my phone out of my pocket. It was from my dad.

Hey Buddy, tried to get your mom a couple times... she didn't call back, sorry.

I began to text him back: I've been kind of—

"Who are you texting?"

"Dad. He wanted to talk to you. Remember?"

She snatched the phone away from me. I should have been focused on why she would do something so weird and random, but I wasn't. No, I was focused on the fact that my not quite a hundred-pound mom who practically needed a booster seat to drive the stupid car had grabbed the phone out of my hands, and I was too tired and weak to even attempt to resist. That's who I was now, someone a Munchkin could push around.

"Give me back my phone."

"No."

"You don't pay for it. Dad does. So you can't take it away."

"Jake, this needs to be about you and me. No one else."

That was weird. I'd never thought of cancer treatment as a mother-son bonding experience. But then I thought, maybe it's not so weird. The way she'd always been about my dad, it kind of made sense she didn't want me talking to him. She'd always wanted me to herself.

For the first time I wondered if maybe their marriage didn't fail because she had ambitions for him. Maybe it failed because she didn't want him around, because she wanted me all to herself. God, that was disturbing to think about. My family was a freaking Greek tragedy.

"You need a therapist," I told her.

"If you live for the next six months, I'll go see one."

"If I don't live six months, you'll need one a lot more."

"But I won't care. I won't want to get better."

"That's really screwed up, Mom. Don't be screwed up."

She laughed. "I wish things in life were that easy. Tell people not to be screwed up, and then they're not."

"Could you at least *try* not to be screwed up?"

With a shrug, she said, "I'll do what I can."

I felt exhausted, which made no sense since all I'd done was sit in a car for like a gazillion hours. "Are we almost there?"

"I think we're getting close. Ten, maybe fifteen minutes."

In my mind, The Godwin Institute was a complex with at least a half-dozen two-story buildings. The fantasy buildings had high windows, were faced in granite, and created an impressive U around a well-kept parking lot. Or better yet, a fountain. I had imagined medical minions parking their cars then going inside to do magical things with syringes and Petri dishes in laboratories the size of football fields. In my mind, The Godwin Institute was the kind of place that needed its own zip code. Given the way my mom was acting, I should have known how wrong I was.

As we pulled up in front, the first thing I noticed was that it was not a complex. It wasn't much more than a hundred-year-old, white-washed wooden building two stories tall with a green-shingled roof and a cupola. I found out later it had once been a Catholic boys' school, and it still had that stern, unhappy look about it. The threat that you might get your knuckles rapped with a ruler seemed to hang in the air. The building cowered on a wide mound with a concrete walkway dissecting the healthy green front lawn.

I want to tell you that it was pitch dark, and I didn't see a thing until the whole horrific building was exposed by a craggy bolt of lightning, but it didn't happen that way. It was a little after seven in the evening and since it was the middle of summer, it was completely light out. So the whole arrival seemed weirdly normal. Well, normal-ish.

Across the street was a shaggy patch of beach and view of Lake Michigan that seemed to go on forever. My mom had pulled up along the curb-less curb and parked. I noticed a couple of other cars parked farther down.

"Don't they have a parking lot?"

"I don't see one, do you?" She got out of the car and went around to the back and opened the cargo door.

I stayed in my seat sitting on the two folded-up bath towels. I'd been away from Chicago exactly half a day and already I missed narrow streets and concrete and confined, controlled landscaping. In the last hour, we'd seen more trees than I'd seen in the last two years.

Not that we didn't have actual wooded areas out in the burbs. We did. It's just that they only went on for a few blocks. Here and there. And they called them "green spaces." Northern Michigan seemed to be nothing but "green spaces." And I could see the huge "green space" behind the Institute. A stand of thirty to forty-foot tall trees sulked at the back of the property, wild and poorly behaved, like a lurking gang of resentful teenagers straight off the CW.

Our neighbors in Niles had the restraint to have one or maybe two trees on their lots. These people, these Michiganders, let trees and underbrush grow at will into a random, riotous sea of green. I missed the control and order of cities, of suburbs.

I missed parking lots.

I struggled out of the seat belt and, with more effort than I'd like to admit, pushed the car door open. I shuffled around to the back of the Rav-4. My mom had taken out the two bags she'd packed for me.

"It's late. Do you think Dr. Harry will see us?" I asked.

"I'm sure he's gone for the day."

"Gone?" I blurted out. "Then why are we here? Why don't we go to a hotel?" I really wanted to lie down and watch something on cable. I wondered if she'd booked herself into a hotel that had the Food Network.

"Jake, you're staying here. I'm staying at a bed and breakfast."

"But—" Tears came to my eyes and I felt ridiculous. I was a nineteen-year-old man, or at least a semi-man, who couldn't spend the night alone without his mother. How pathetic was that? But then I thought about the *me* I'd seen in the mirror at the rest area. I was going to die. I was going to die soon. Maybe even that night. And my mom was dropping me off. Leaving me. With strangers. I might die and never see her again. And she still had my phone. I might die and never get to text my dad back.

Suddenly, I was pissed off. I wanted to be at home. I wanted to spend some normal time with my mom, even though I doubted she'd be able to pull that off. I wanted to see my dad and my stepmom, and I even wanted to see the steplings and the halflings. I wanted to die in my own life. Not in some strange research institute with bad landscaping.

"Jake. This is what we need to do to make you better."

I looked at her and said something I should have said hours before. "I have a fever. It's really high."

five

She didn't believe me, which I guess should not have been a surprise. It was clear I didn't want to stay there, and a fever might land me in a real hospital or at least sleeping on the sofa at her bed and breakfast so she could keep an eye on me. Standing on tippy toe she put a hand onto my forehead and left it there for only a moment.

"Okay. It does feel high. Very high."

"Use the GPS on my phone. Find a hospital." Of course, she had her own phone, but if she used mine, I might be able to get her to give it back.

Walking to the front of the car, she grabbed her purse off the front seat. She was digging through it when she got back to me. Abruptly she stopped, bit her lip, and said, "Jake, we're here. All we need to do is go inside. Leave the bags. I'll get them later."

"But you said the doctor was gone?"

"I'm sure someone can help us." She reached over, pulled my arm around her shoulders, and began to lead me up the front walk. I wanted to tell her I was really fine, and I could walk on my own, but the reality was I couldn't. I had to lean on her, so I didn't end up facedown on the sidewalk. It was all I could do not to sprawl out in the soft-looking grass. I wanted to lie down that bad.

"Sleep called to me, and so did its inhospitable cousin, death." That thought made me giggle. It sounded Shakespearean. As though I was some poor tortured character rising up from the pile of dead people who littered Act Five, Scene Next to Last to utter my final words.

"What are you talking about?"

"Did I say that out loud?"

"Yes, you were talking about sleep and death."

"I'm tired. It was just a thought scampering across my brain like a squirrel about to scoot up a tree." I giggled again. My thoughts were getting weird, probably because they were scampering.

"I don't think you're getting enough oxygen to your brain," she said, pushing the double doors open. Inside, a nurse sat at an enormous, antique mahogany reception desk. To one side was a wide arch, through which I glimpsed a ward with empty beds. To the other side, a couple of doors. Beyond the desk was a flight of stairs that led to a landing and, presumably, the second floor.

The nurse was in her late forties, with ashen hair tucked into a tight, torturous bun. She wore a dingy gray cardigan and a frown so sour I thought it must hurt.

"Are you the Margates?" she asked crisply. "We were expecting you hours—"

"He's sick. Fever. Can you call the doctor?"

A floor-to-ceiling stained glass window dominated the landing, catching most of my attention as my mother haggled with the nurse. The window depicted Jesus Christ, draped in a sheet, the wound in his scrawny side clearly visible. He held a staff with some kind of banner or flag on it. We were not religious people, my mom and I, but even I knew it was the resurrection. Christ called back from the dead. He was an unhappy looking Christ, gray, gaunt. I had the funny thought that he looked like me. The *me* I'd seen at the rest stop. I saw my face floating over his and knew I was detaching, letting go of reality. I wasn't sad about it. It wasn't such a great reality, after all.

Even though I was still leaning on her, my mom seemed far away as she explained to the nurse what was going on with me. The explanation seemed to be taking a super long time.

I sped things along by fainting dead away.

six

No idea how long I was out. I came to on a vinyl-covered examining table. Someone had adjusted it so my head was elevated. I couldn't see the rest of the room behind me or even any of the room. All I could see was a handsome man of about sixty hovering a few inches above me. His hair, which there was a lot of, was salt-and-pepper, though mainly salt. He wore a badly trimmed beard and thick, smudged, black-framed glasses. His face was absolutely symmetrical, each feature perfectly formed and exactly the right size. *He must have been incredibly good-looking when he was young,* I thought. His faded beauty hung over him like a shroud.

Seeing I'd opened my eyes, he frowned. "You have a severe infection. I'm not sure where. I'm not sure it matters. We've put you on an antibiotic drip which is already helping you." He stepped back, and I saw an intravenous line going into the back of my hand.

"I have a Hickman line," I said. "Why didn't you—"

"Yes, I know. That could be the cause of your infection. We'll be taking that out tomorrow or the next day."

"Who are you?"

"Dr. Harry."

"No. You're not here."

"I heard you were in trouble. I came back."

"You have a silly name." I didn't exactly mean to say that, it just came out. Things in my head were still kind of wonky.

"I can assure you the silliness of my name was made apparent to me decades ago in grade school. And college. And medical school. And many times since." There was no trace of humor in his voice. He studied a machine sitting slightly behind me and then readjusted a clip on my finger. "I don't think you're getting enough oxygen. Do you feel light-headed?"

"For the last five years."

He stepped over to the door and opened it. "Miss Haggerty, could you get an oxygen setup from storage?"

As he did that, I had a moment to look around. Windows on one wall looked out at the front. It was darker now, but not so dark I couldn't see my mom's Rav-4 down at the curb-less curb. My bags were still sitting on the ground behind it. The opposite wall was lined with cabinets and a counter with a small sink. Next to the door was a mirror or mirrored cabinet, whichever. I could see my mom standing behind me. The look on her face was the one she got when I made her watch horror movies.

She caught me looking at her. "Just try to relax." I could have said the same to her. "The antibiotic should improve things soon."

Dr. Harry turned and said, "I think we should begin Jake's treatment tonight."

"Tonight?" I blurted. "But, I mean, when I've had chemo before the doctor's wanted to make sure...um, I need to be healthy. Or, you know, healthi-*er*."

"Perhaps it *is* better to wait until he's stable," my mother added.

"You're assuming he's going to become stable. I think that's unlikely. If he dies tonight, then we've lost our chance." It was the verbal equivalent of a bucket of cold water. Two actually. One for my mom and one for me. This was not the way doctors talked to us. Doctors talked about whether they were optimistic or not optimistic. They talked about percentiles and success rates. They didn't say things like, "if he dies tonight."

I was stunned for a moment, and I assumed my mother was, too. I couldn't see her because she'd moved, but she was still somewhere behind me. Her silence meant she was taken aback. Finally, I heard her say, "Yes, all right. Go ahead."

"Actually, it's not up to you. Your son is of age, and he's conscious. He needs to be the one making decisions about his health."

Shit. Why did I have to be conscious? Dying was easier when you didn't have to be the one making decisions. In fact, it was really easy if you weren't even there. I kind of wanted to pass out again. Instead, I forced myself to focus on the dilemma at hand. The doctor wanted to give me something that might—though probably wouldn't— save my life or might —and probably would—end my life.

On the one hand, I wasn't sure it mattered either way. On the other hand, it mattered a whole lot to my mom who'd already decided I should take the treatment. If I said no, she'd spend whatever was left of my short life trying to convince me to take whatever the treatment turned out to be. And if I never took it and died, she'd blame herself for not convincing me. That left me without much choice. Or did it? It was *my* life. What did I want? Could it really save me? And did I want to do whatever I had to do to make that happen?

I don't know whether he picked up on my dilemma or not, but Dr. Harry said to my mom, "It would be better if you'd wait outside."

"No, it wouldn't be. He's my son. Jake, you want me here, don't you?" My mom asked as she came around to face me. She looked so scared and worried I realized there was another hand I hadn't even thought about. What if I took the treatment and it killed me? My mom had been pushing for me to do it. She might blame herself. Shit. Now I had a dilemma with three hands. Which might have been funny if they didn't mostly end with me being dead.

"It's okay, Mom. I can make the decision."

"No, Jake you need me—"

"You should go check into your B&B. You don't want to lose your room."

"No! What if—?"

"Don't fight with me. I'm sick, okay? The doctor just said the treatment will keep me alive."

Actually, he'd only implied that, but he didn't correct me the way most doctors would have. Instead, he took that as my agreement to take the treatment.

"I'll go get everything we need. I'll be back in a minute or two."

When he was gone, I took my mom's hand and said, "I want to do this. Whatever happens it's on me."

"I'm your mom. Whatever happens is on *me*. It's always on me."

"I don't want you to blame yourself."

"Then live. If you're alive, there's no reason to blame anyone."

God she's stubborn, I thought. At that particular moment I really hoped there was no such thing as guilt after death because she'd just saddled me with a ton of it. "Go check into your B&B. I promise not to die. How's that?"

"I don't know, Jake."

"Go. Get some sleep. Come back in the morning."

I don't know why I wanted her to go so badly. I mean, I'd been pissed she was planning to leave me all alone. Even I could see I'd changed my mind pretty quick. But one thing I'd learned about being ill was that sometimes when a thing actually happened, you didn't want what you thought you'd want. Now that it was entirely possible I was about to die, I wasn't sure I wanted to do it in front of my mom. In fact, I sort of knew I didn't want to do it in front of her.

I'd imagined my death all sorts of ways. Kind of like my life was some weird Syfy series with three or four different endings. And my mom was always there in my imagination. But so were a lot of other people. She wasn't alone. We weren't in some strange place, and I was leaving her with people who liked her, at least a little. People who'd take care of her. I'd never thought about dying with just her there. That seemed mean. Or rude. Or I don't know just wrong.

My mom took her phone out of her purse. "I'll just call the B&B. Tell them I'm going to be late. That was a good idea, Jake." She did that a lot. Pretended that her ideas were actually my ideas. She frowned at the phone. "I'm not getting service."

I almost said she deserved that for taking my phone away. Instead, I said, "Just go there. Come back in the morning. I'll be here. I promise."

After a few deep breaths, she gave in, practically crawled onto the table so she could kiss me on the cheek and hurried out of the room. I felt like I could read her mind. She was worried she'd never see me again. She had good reason to be.

SEVEN

Miss Haggerty and her tight, scary bun came into the room with an oxygen tank, miscellaneous tubes, and a mask. It took only a few moments to get me set up, but I was anxious the whole time. Until you get sick, you don't spend much time thinking about how much you actually love oxygen, so let me just say, *oxygen is freaking amazing*. Taking a deep breath of oxygen after your body has been underperforming for hours and hours is better than any drug they sell on the streets. Not that I've tried many of those, but you get the drift. Oxygen is amazing *and* addictive.

"How is that?" she asked. "Is it comfortable?"

It wasn't, but it never was at first. "It's good."

"We have cannulas, but Dr. Harry likes to start with the mask."

"So this happens a lot? People come in and faint?"

"No." I thought she might scold me for being inconsiderate. "You're the first to try that trick. But we have others who go on and off oxygen." Then she added, "I'll be right outside if you need me."

Her look told me it would be better if I didn't, though.

After a couple of minutes, my mind began to function better. Or, you know, just function. I was alone in a very odd place recommended on the Internet. I didn't have my phone. I should have asked my mother to give it back but even if she had, it probably wouldn't work since I had the same provider as my mom. If her reception sucked, so would mine.

And then Dr. Harry came back in carrying the kind of small bag you use for shaving stuff. He took out a single vial and held it up to the light. The fluid was clear. It could have been water. It could have been vodka. It could have been any one of the half dozen treatments that had already been tried on me. All my treatments had looked the same. Clear. When I'd been infused, as they called it, I'd seen other people get colorful chemo. Red or blue or yellow. I always wanted to do that sometime. Pick my chemo by color. I'd probably pick blue, although red had a certain appeal. The side effects were probably more dramatic.

Dr. Harry shut down the IV line and undid the bag of antibiotics dripping into me. I was a little concerned about that. I'd thought I'd be getting the treatment *and* the antibiotics. It wouldn't be the first time I've had multiple medications dripped into me at once.

Lifting the mask off my face, I asked, "So, what is it you're giving me? Does it have one of those names that sounds like a word but isn't a word? Like Cluvada or Humidron or Loyaida?"

"This doesn't have a name yet. We just call it Property Five."

"What happened to properties one through four?"

"They didn't work. That's what science is. Trial and error."

I thought to ask him how many people had been given Property Five, but to be honest, I wasn't sure I wanted to know. If it were under a hundred, I'd be taking my life into my hands. And if I was taking that kind of risk, I didn't want to know it. *Shit,* I thought, *look around.* Look where you are. I didn't think the place was big enough to hold a hundred participants. Dr. Harry hadn't given Property Five to a hundred people. I'd be lucky if he'd given it to twenty.

"What does it do?" I slipped the mask back onto my face and inhaled deeply.

He looked at me for a moment as though he was deciding whether or not to tell me. Then he made his decision. "Most cancer therapies attack fast-growing cells. They don't distinguish between the fast-growing cancer cells and your body's own fast-growing cells. That's why certain side effects are common: hair loss, nausea. Hair is made up of fast-growing cells. So is the intestinal lining."

I nodded. This wasn't exactly news to me. I'd spent a lot of time killing exactly those cells. He took a moment to unclamp the IV line. Property Five began to drip into me.

Here we go, I thought.

Dr. Harry continued, "Different cancer treatments affect different parts of a cell. Property Five works on the microtubules."

Okay, that was new. No one had ever talked about those before, whatever they were. He left a pause for me to say I didn't understand. Which was pretty smart since I kind of didn't.

"The last thing I remember in science class is homeostasis," I said, leaving the mask on. The oxygen was too precious. And it helped with homeostasis.

"Seventh grade science. Our educational system leaves much to be desired." He frowned for a moment as though he were actually thinking about how to fix that but then continued, "Microtubules are in some ways the skeletal structure of a cell. Though they're more complicated than that. They're involved in many of a cell's processes. So, you see anything you do to change their makeup changes a cell's behavior."

"You mean, like the cancer cells die."

"Yes. Without microtubules cancer cells die."

I lifted the mask. "Thanks for explaining all that. I kind of understand." Or at least I thought I did. My guess was that he'd dumbed it down a lot, which was why he seemed to be so careful with what he said.

"How long does it take to go through this bag?"

"About two hours. Do you want to switch to the cannula?"

"That would probably be good."

"I'm going to step out. I'll send Miss Haggerty in to do that."

Without a nod or a goodbye or even a friendly smile, Dr. Harry walked out of the room. He seemed like a really stiff guy. For some reason, I hoped I lived long enough to make him laugh. I wondered if I should try and sleep. Sleep was supposed to be healthy, and there certainly wasn't anything else to do. I was stuck there for the next few hours, at least.

I closed my eyes. Ready to sleep. But adrenaline raced through my veins right next to this new poison. What if it worked? What if Property Five actually saved me? What would I do with my life? It had been so long since I'd thought about having a life that I really had no idea. The question was uncomfortable. I didn't want to think about what I might do if I had a life in front of me. If I thought about having a life, I'd want one. I'd want to make those dreams come true. Or at least try. And there was still a very big, very real possibility that Property Five would fail.

I didn't want to hope where there was no hope.

Even with the oxygen, my breathing grew worse. I think ten minutes passed. Maybe more. I began to wonder if Miss Haggerty was coming back or if she'd just decided to ignore me. I struggled to take a deep breath, except it didn't feel deep. It felt like someone had stuffed my lungs with cotton balls. I was breathing, but it was having little effect.

Finally, she came into the room carrying a cannula in a clear plastic bag. She smelled like cigarette smoke, which maybe explained why she'd taken so long. Had to have her ciggie break. She walked around the table to the IV stand and checked it. I heard her say, "Huh."

"What's the matter?"

"Did Dr. Harry say why he stopped the antibiotic?"

"He felt it was a good idea to get the Property Five started. Is that not right?"

The frown on her face told me maybe it wasn't. I was pretty sure he could have given me both at once. So, why hadn't he?

"I'm sure it's fine. Dr. Harry knows what he's doing," she said, remaining expressionless. She opened the plastic bag to get to the cannula.

"Can you increase the oxygen first? I can't breathe."

She reached down and fiddled with the oxygen canister. Then she began switching me over to the cannula. There was only a moment or two between the time she took the mask off me and when she managed to get the cannula into place but still, I began to gasp. My mouth opened wide, and my neck strained as though either of those things would help me get air into my thickening lungs. Neither did. Panic filled me. I wanted to run but knew I couldn't even get off the table.

Miss Haggerty's face paled. She got swimmy and swirly, then she stopped having outlines and sort of blurred into the room. I reached out, for what I'm not sure.

"I'd better get Dr. Harry," she said, fleeing the room.

I stared at the ceiling, trying to focus, struggling for breath, my heart racing as though I was being chased. Bracing myself on the table, I pulled and pulled for air. The ceiling was made of acoustic tile. It had been painted the same putty color as the walls. I wondered if it dampened sound, if patients—the ones not struggling to breathe—had screamed in that room and not been heard.

The door popped open, and Dr. Harry rushed in, Miss Haggerty behind him. He ignored me, going right for the IV stand. I thought he might change it out and put the bag of antibiotic fluid back on in hopes of bringing the infection back under control. Instead, he played with the clamp until the drip was constant. My hand began to burn. He turned and unlocked a drawer. Moments later he gave me a shot in the upper arm.

Though I was struggling, light-headed, darkness closing in, I managed, "Wha—"

"Prednisone. It will help open the airways," Dr. Harry said.

I felt faint. Nauseated. Things went gray, then black—

—then I was looking down at the room, as though I was floating near the ceiling, as though I was taking in the scene from a security camera. Except the quality was good. Really good. I could see everything in a super realistic way. And I was calm. My breathless panic had passed.

Looking at myself on the table, I was almost blue and it didn't look like I was breathing. Miss Haggerty was tense. Dr. Harry intense. But I didn't care. It was nice on the ceiling. Up there with the putty-colored tile.

"Doctor, he's not breathing."

"Check his pulse."

Miss Haggerty felt around my wrist. I knew before she did she wouldn't find anything. My heart wasn't beating. I wasn't breathing. I felt relief. As though I'd been pretending to be alive for a very long time, and now I didn't have to pretend anymore.

"I'm not getting a pulse," she said. I barely heard her. I was thinking about my mom. She would feel bad, but she would feel bad no matter what. Maybe this final effort, this trip to The Godwin Institute to save me would help her find peace. She'd tried. She'd tried very hard. What more could she have done? Would she find solace in that? I hoped she would.

Miss Haggerty was pushing on my chest. I knew what that was called from TV, now what was it? Compressions. She was doing compressions. They looked painful. I was glad I wasn't going to wake up to cracked ribs. I waited for a white light to appear. For a tunnel. I didn't expect to see anyone I knew. I didn't know a lot of dead people.

Not much happened.

I watched as Dr. Harry ordered Miss Haggerty to stop the compressions so he could give me a shot. I could see where it might be difficult to find a vein when someone was pounding on the patient's chest. I felt bad for them. It must feel shitty to lose a patient. Like it's your fault, even though it's not.

People work that way a lot, blaming themselves for stupid stuff they couldn't do anything about while totally letting themselves off the hook for things they could have easily changed.

Dr. Harry opened the cabinet and pulled out a portable defibrillator. They were going to shock me. I knew it wasn't going to work. I was too dead to be revived. But it was still interesting to watch. Things weren't happening like they do on TV. Dr. Harry didn't yell "Clear!" like a TV doctor. It wasn't even dramatic. He seemed almost bored. He pulled up my shirt and put the paddles on me. Snapped at Miss Haggerty to "Get back."

I watched my body flop on the table. Haggerty cowered by the counter—okay, she was dramatic. She actually looked scared. There was a pause, the doctor fiddled with the defibrillator and shocked me again. Nothing happened, and I was glad. I'd be able to move on soon. All of this would be over. It would be behind me. Whatever came next was about to come. And I wanted it.

And then suddenly there was nothing but dark and pain and more dark.

eight

Clawing my way out of a thick, soupy darkness, I came to in a large room with several hospital beds. Ten, actually, though I didn't know that at first. Counting shit was not the first thing on my very fuzzy mind. What was on my mind was trying to figure out if I was alive or not.

On the one hand, I felt pretty crappy, so I was probably alive. Presumably, death was painless. God, I hoped death was painless. To be dead and in pain would suck. On the other hand, the room was eerie bright and everything around me seemed to glow. That was kind of tipping the scale toward my not being alive.

Not to mention, I was extremely cold. Another check mark on the side of death. My hand itched where the IV went in, the room smelled of antiseptic cleaner, my chest hurt like a mother. Ribs aching where they'd been cracked—shit, I'd hoped to miss out on that—and there was stinging where my Hickman line went in. I reached up and felt around with one hand and found the line gone. Why was it gone? I sort of remembered Dr. Harry saying he wanted to take it out but wasn't that going to be in a few days? I couldn't remember exactly. It seemed important for a moment and then didn't.

Trying to sit up, I saw three of the four walls had windows. They were partly open, and fresh air drifted casually into the room. I could see the lake out the window; it was blue and serene. On the side of the building was a stand of trees and someone's dilapidated garage. The window behind me, nearest my bed, had a couple of flies clinging to screen, trying to find a way in.

On the other side of my bed, in a molded-plastic chair, sat a guy around my age, maybe a year or so younger, with the most amazing brown eyes I'd ever seen. He had thick dark hair, an impish smile, pale skin with a bluish tint, and incredibly long eyelashes. Like everything else in the room, he seemed to glow making me wonder if he was an angel.

"Am I dead?" I asked.

"I hope not. It's kind of dull around here. I'm counting on you to liven things up." I couldn't imagine myself livening anything up, but it was kind of nice that someone thought I could.

"Who are you?"

"Goth."

"What?"

"It's short for Goliath. Goliath Gunderson. Goth."

"Seriously, your parents named you Goliath?"

"It's biblical."

"Not in a good way." Suddenly, I felt like maybe I shouldn't have said that. "I mean, you've probably heard that before."

"Yeah, a few times. I'm going to change it someday. I just can't decide between Brian or Dave. Which do you think is more boring?"

I couldn't tell if he was kidding. Or mocking me. Or both. All I really wanted to do, though, was lie back down and drift off into the dark of sleep. But Goth was staring at me, so it would be rude to drift off.

"My name is Jake. Jake Margate." I felt a bit embarrassed about having such a regular sounding name.

"I know your name. Dr. Harry told me you were coming."

"Oh, all right. Are you in the study?"

He nodded.

"So you've already gotten Property Five?"

"No. Not yet. Dr. Harry says I'm not ready."

I wondered what that meant. Why was I ready and Goth wasn't? He certainly looked like he was doing better than I was, at least at that particular moment. "How long have you been here?"

"A week, ten days, something like that. It's hard to keep track. So what do you like to do for fun?"

I had no idea how to answer that question, so I said the first thing that popped into my head. "Breathe."

And then, to prove my point I took a deep breath. Or tried to, anyway. The breath I managed was shallow, and my lungs still felt as though they were filled with cotton balls. And moving my chest hurt like hell. Obviously, I still had a lung infection. It hadn't just gone away overnight. However, it didn't seem to matter as much. There was a cannula on my upper lip. They must have the oxygen levels turned up to the max since I didn't feel panicked or oxygen starved. I barely felt the need to breathe at all, which was good.

I noticed Goth nodding his head. "Yeah, breathing is the best."

There was something about him that seemed familiar, but I was sure I'd never seen him before. Too tired to keep sitting up, I lay back down and said, "I thought you were an angel when I woke up."

"Sorry to disappoint."

"I'm not..." Sleep was creeping up on me, like a slimy creature from a lagoon.

"You're not what?"

"Disappointed."

ninE

The next time I woke up, it was my mom sitting in the molded-plastic chair. She was watching old episodes of *Devious Maids* on my iPad.

"There you are," she said when she saw that I was awake.

I found the remote control for the bed lying next to my hand. I raised myself up so I could get a better look at the room. It looked to have been two separate rooms now joined together. The walls were painted in the same putty color as the examining room. The floor was thick wooden slats painted gray. It had a very odd, old-timey feeling for a hospital. But then I reminded myself it wasn't a hospital. It was a research institute.

At the far end of the room was an archway through which I could see the reception area and the pink-sweatered back and shoulders of the day nurse. Five beds lined each side of the room. The other beds were empty and stripped except for two on the opposite side of the room. Those held a couple of very elderly men, each surrounded by machines monitoring bodily functions. Neither man seemed to be conscious.

None of what I saw was what I was looking for. "Where's Goth?"

My mother scrunched up her face. "Goth? What's a Goth?"

"It's short for Goliath."

"No one would name a child Goliath. That's cruel."

I couldn't disagree with her. "I thought he was an angel. I thought I was dead."

"You're nowhere near dead. They said you had a rough night, though. I'm sorry I wasn't here. I shouldn't have left. But here's the wonderful part —Dr. Harry is absolutely certain the treatment worked."

"Why? Why does he think that?"

"Because he's the doctor."

That didn't make sense. Why would a doctor be absolutely certain something worked after less than twenty-four hours? Was the fact that I was still alive proof that Property Five had worked? That was crazy. Cancer drugs took weeks to prove effective. Months. Years even.

"I don't think Goth was an angel. I think he was real."

"I'm sure he *is* real. There's another ward on the other side of the building and a whole second floor. Or he could be outside. It's a big property. Lots of places to hide a boy named Goth."

I hadn't expected that. I'd expected her to tell me I was dreaming.

"What's the rest of the Institute like?"

"I haven't seen much. There's the reception area, which you got a look at before you fainted. And the exam room we were in. And the ward on the other side of the building, of course. And there's the upstairs. Dr. Harry mentioned testing. I think that's upstairs. Oh, I almost forgot, there's a solarium in the back. Dr. Harry took me there to talk. It's lovely."

"They took out my Hickman."

"You're not going to need it." She clicked off the TV show and gave me an extra big smile, something I hadn't seen in a long time. I gave her the side-eye.

"I'm cold. Can I have another blanket?"

"Sorry. I had enough trouble getting them to give you this one." This one was thin, hardly a blanket at all "They're lowering your temperature on purpose. It's part of the treatment."

"Huh? Why?"

"I don't know exactly. You know how doctors are. They don't like to tell you things."

I stared at her. This was my mother who'd known everything about my treatment for the last five years. "You let him get away with not telling you?"

"Dr. Harry got you through the night. I wasn't going to look a gift horse in the mouth." The relief in her voice was palpable. She must have been pretty sure I was going to die when I'd made her leave. "And you shouldn't either. Just do everything you're told, and you'll get better. And isn't that the only thing that matters?"

I'm going to get better? Things were barely making sense. "Didn't you at least google whatever it is?"

She pursed her lips at me. "No. I didn't. I trust Dr. Harry. Besides, there's no cell service here and no wi-fi. If you insist, I'll do it when I get back to the B&B."

Something was wrong. I couldn't figure out what, though. "How is the B&B?"

"Nice enough. I slept about two hours. Now that I know you're okay, I'm going to go back and get some real sleep."

I heard the day nurse singing a Lady GaGa song under her breath, except she was turning it into a country song. Which was weird. And lame. What was weirder was that I glanced over at the reception area, and she wasn't at the desk anymore. In fact, I couldn't see her anywhere. So, how could I hear her? What was that about? Was I hallucinating or something? I looked at my mother with enough confusion on my face to make her ask, "What? Is something wrong?"

"I can hear singing. Can you hear singing?"

"Hmmm?" She listened. "Well, maybe. You know these old buildings. Full of drafts. This used to be a boy's school. Catholic, I think. Wait, now I hear it."

And just as she said it, the day nurse came into the ward pushing a vitals stand in front of her, still humming her strange hybrid tune. She must have gone to retrieve the stand from a supply closet somewhere. Maybe my mom was right, maybe there was a vent or—

"Good morning, sweetie! I'm Nurse Margie," she said when she got to my bed. She wore a blue pair of scrubs with a pink, stretched-out cardigan tugged over them. It had yarn flowers attached randomly on the front. Her hair was dyed a red that made her pale skin attractive. Otherwise, she had done little to improve her rather ordinary looks.

"It's time for your vital signs again."

Again? I didn't remember doing them before. I wondered how many times we'd done them since I got there. She stuck a plastic-covered thermometer into my mouth.

"It's nice to see you're finally awake." She smiled at my mom. They'd already met at some point. Then she put the blood pressure cuff around my arm. As the cuff inflated, she took the thermometer out and released the plastic covering into a nearby wastepaper basket.

"How low is my temperature?"

"Ninety-five point eight. Oh, fudge, I'm not supposed to—" She bit her lip and smiled at me, and then at my mom. "Raw data can be confusing to a patient. I mean, that's what Dr. Harry said."

"I'm sure it sounds much worse than it is," my mother said.

Ninety-five degrees was warm if you were a pebble on a beach. If you're a person, it's the deep freeze. "I'm from Chicago so I'm kind of used to the cold," I said. "But shouldn't I be shivering my ass off."

"I had to read up on that," she admitted. "It's called medical hypothermia. This solution I'm giving you is, I think, a bunch of different drugs. One of them shuts down the body's defenses against the cold. Like shivering. See, that's why you're not shivering your, um, butt off. Dr. Harry said they've been using it for years in Europe. Oh double fudge, there I am giving you raw data again. Anyway, you've only got a few more hours of it."

Nurse Margie took the cuff off. "Blood pressure low, heart rate low. Dr. Harry said to expect that with this medication. Nothing to worry about." She looked at me and paled a bit. She shouldn't have told me that either.

"Thank you," my mother said.

Pushing the vitals stand in front of her, Nurse Margie scurried off.

"Well, it's been a long time since we've heard that," my mother said.

"Heard what?"

"'Nothing to worry about.'"

And she was right. I couldn't remember the last time a medical professional had used those words. Just the idea made me sleepy. "Nothing to worry about." Could it be true? Could there really be nothing to worry about? And then before I could even finish the thought, I was sleeping.

ten

—remember to mark the calendar. Yesterday was a remarkable day. One of the most remarkable of my life. Any life. All lives. Someday, people will look at the date and know it was the day Dr. Ronald Harry changed the way we think about life. No, no, that's wrong. This is not about self-aggrandizement. They'll remember yesterday simply as the day things changed. Yes, that's better. History can leave my name out of it. I haven't worked all my life for fame. There are more important things."

The office was cramped. A desk, a chair, and two filing cabinets crowded together on one side of the room, while a sofa stretched from one wall to the other opposite. On the desk was a computer. I knew Dr. Harry could have been recording himself on the computer, videoing himself if he wanted, but he was using his smartphone to record, holding it like a microphone in front of his chin.

"Let's see, I should get the facts down. The subject was given Property Five at approximately eight thirty-eight on the evening of the fourteenth. Forty-five minutes later, the subject suffered a cardiac event. CPR was administered. Then defibrillation. Rhythm was restored. We continued to administer Property Five until the complete treatment was given."

On the walls were his diplomas, five or six of them from different universities. Among them were photos of young men in their twenties, thirties. I had the fleeting thought that Dr. Harry might like younger guys, but then I realized the photos were from before I was born. They looked like the pictures my mom had from when she was a little girl. The guys were kind of hot. The photos were taken in apartments at Christmas, on beaches in the summer, in front of important looking buildings. One of the guys was obviously Dr. Harry. I was right. He'd been super good-looking like thirty years ago.

But wait. Was I right? I was dreaming, wasn't I? I mean, I had to be dreaming. I was doing the ceiling thing again. Looking down at Dr. Harry. CCTV. That's what they called it on British cop shows. They had CCTV everywhere. I had it in my dreams.

"During the night, subject was kept in a hypothermic state. Vital signs remain inhibited but steady just as expected. Secondary treatment, provided by Callabray Labs, has begun, and the subject is responding well. Very encouraging, very exciting. If the subject continues to respond... No, when the subject continues to respond well. There is no room for doubt. Doubt is the enemy of hope. As the subject continues to respond, secondary treatments will be reduced though it is expected that some form of treatment will be required on an ongoing basis, not unlike the type of medical support required by transplant patients. A small price to pay for—"

eleven

I woke to find Dr. Harry standing over me glaring into my face. Behind the wrinkles and puffiness, I could see the young man in the photos, the man he'd once been. Except that had to be wrong. Backwards. I'd dreamed the photos. The dream was a side effect of treatment. It had to be.

'Patient may experience vivid dreams, weightlessness, and a sense of being disembodied, which may be accompanied by detailed, probably incorrect information about individuals the patient barely knows.' Wow, the lawyers were going to have to haggle about how to add that to the end of a TV commercial.

"Where's my mom?" My voice was groggier than I'd ever heard it

"I believe she's napping at her hotel."

"B&B. She's staying at a B&B."

"Mmmmhmmm," he said. I could tell he didn't care where she was staying. She could be sleeping in her car for all it mattered to him.

"I had a dream about you," I said. "You were talking into your phone. I dreamed I was in your office. You used to have friends."

"The nurse was just here. You probably heard me talking to her."

I shook my head. "It didn't sound like that."

It wasn't real. Why did I think it was real? Dr. Harry didn't seem the sort to be emotional, but he'd been excited in the dream, almost happy. I

45

barely knew him, but it was hard to imagine him being those things. Though that's what I'd done. I'd imagined him happy.

"You're right. I used to have friends. I still have friends, though not as many."

Using two fingers, he spread the lids on my right eye as wide as he could. He shined a penlight into it and looked the eyeball over thoroughly. It kind of hurt, and I couldn't help but try to squint a little.

"Hold still." Then he repeated the annoying process with my left eye.

"We have to stop meeting like this," I said. It was a joke. A very old joke. The kind of thing someone would say in some ancient movie from like the eighties. He didn't crack a smile. His face was tense. He was looking for something, but I had no idea what. He took his fingers out of my eye and seemed to relax.

"Your eyes look good."

"There's never been anything wrong with my eyes."

"You have clear, healthy eyes."

I glanced around the ward. We were alone. Well, except for the two old men laying inert and comatose across the room, we were alone. I was tempted to ask about them. What were they doing here? Where had they come from? Why weren't they in a nursing home? But I bit my tongue and played the good patient.

Still, I couldn't help asking, "So my prognosis is good?"

"It is. But I'm sure your mother told you that."

"I thought it might be nice to hear it from you. You *are* the doctor."

He nodded. "It's going to be a long road. But you'll make it."

"What's going to happen on that long road?"

"I don't know. We'll find out together."

He was a doctor, but a strange one. Doctors didn't say, "I don't know." I couldn't remember another time I'd heard a doctor say that. I'd heard "I don't know my schedule next week." Or "I don't know if we validate parking." But I'd never heard "I don't know what the course of your disease will be." That just didn't happen. And "We'll find out together" that was just bizarre.

"Can you sit up?" Dr. Harry asked. Without answering, I did. Somewhere along the line I'd been put into a pair of pajamas. I wasn't sure if I'd been wearing them when I fell asleep or if I'd been changed while I was sleeping. Details like that kept slipping away from me.

Next to the bed was a nightstand with a single drawer. Where were my clothes? My mom had been using my iPad, so she'd put them somewhere. And she was probably the one who'd picked out the pajamas I was wearing, something I could have figured out simply from the fact that they were an old pair of *Simpsons* PJs.

They would have been very cool when I was fourteen and trying to watch every single episode of the show, but I'd grown out of that and now it was faintly embarrassing when Dr. Harry unbuttoned the top, separating Homer and Marge to press a stethoscope against my too thin chest. Expecting to feel the icy cold metal of the scope, I was surprised when it wasn't cold. Dr. Harry must have warmed it while I wasn't looking. He moved it around my chest, listening, listening. But then his fingers grazed me, hot and burning.

"Are you okay? Your fin—"

"Don't talk." He moved the scope around a few more times and was satisfied. "Of course, I'm okay. I'm also not the patient, so even if I—"

"It's just that your fingers are really hot. Like you have a fever or something."

"Your temperature is still well below normal. It changes the way you perceive things."

"Oh, that's right...medical hypothermia."

He shot me an unhappy look. Now he was a normal doctor. Doctors were threatened if you knew anything at all about your own disease. I didn't know much about medicine, but I had picked up a few things about acute blah-blah-blah leukemia, and whenever they came out of my mouth, doctors looked annoyed. Just the way Dr. Harry had.

"Why is this place called The Godwin Institute?"

"I named it after someone who meant a great deal to me."

"So, it's yours?"

"Basically."

"I died last night. Didn't I?"

"Of course not." His voice was clipped and stiff. He was lying, I could tell. But then that was probably normal. He'd lost me. I died. Even if it was just for a few minutes, there could be ramifications. I could maybe sue him. People sued over less.

Dr. Harry continued what he was doing. He checked the pulse in both of my wrists, moved up to my neck and checked it there, walked to the bottom of the bed, lifted the blanket, and checked the pulse in both ankles. Then he moved back to the middle of the bed to pull the blanket down to my knees. He slipped a hand between my thighs just below my crotch. He pressed a finger against one thigh and felt around. Then he did the other thigh.

I could feel blood in my cheeks. I wondered for a second if he was a pedo, but quickly rejected the idea. He had his hand in my crotch and looked kind of bored. He glanced up at me. "You're blushing. That's good." I didn't think so. I thought it was humiliating. I mean, yeah, he was a doctor but come on...

He removed his hand from my thigh and moved up to palpate my stomach—which is a kind of medical tickling.

"Your circulation is good."

It couldn't have been that good. If I were healthy, all his poking around would have produced something more embarrassing than a blush. I mean, he was an old guy and all, but I was nineteen and the places he'd been poking around...

During my occasional spurts of almost-health, certain parts of my anatomy had been super active whether the rest of me was interested or not. Seriously, giving a teenager a boner is no great accomplishment. So, the fact that I hadn't risen to the occasion said more about my circulation than he had.

"There is some bloating in the abdomen." He made a note in my file and said, more to himself, "The antibiotics should take care of that."

I reached down and pulled the blanket over me. "How long do I have to be here?"

"I don't know. As long as it takes."

"As long as what takes?"

"As long as it takes to make you a hundred percent healthy." Normally, when a doctor said something like that, he smiled. Dr. Harry didn't. I wondered if he maybe used Botox. He kept his face that still. Then he added, "I'd like to begin aggressive testing tomorrow."

"Aggressive? What does that mean?"

"Blood work. EEG. PET scan. The blood work will be daily. The imaging every other day. "

"So, where do I go for those?" I asked.

"We have all the necessary equipment here."

"Oh."

It seemed odd they'd have that kind of stuff. I mean, it was expensive. I began to worry about how much all of this was costing. It was obviously experimental. Was my mom's insurance even paying for this? I didn't want to bankrupt her. My dad would offer to help, but she was too proud. Of course, if I stayed long enough, I could bankrupt my dad, too.

Dr. Harry took a step as though to leave.

"Um, are they going to bring me something to eat soon?" If I was bankrupting my parents, I might as well get a good meal out of it.

"Are you hungry?"

I thought about it. I wasn't. I wasn't hungry at all. "No, I guess not."

"I'd like you to hold off until you actually feel hunger."

"But shouldn't I try to eat? To keep up my strength." God, I'd heard that one from my mother so many times I could barely believe I was saying it.

"There's glucose in the IV fluids. Among other things. You'll be fine."

Mmmmm. Glucose. Yum.

twelve

My mom came back just after dinnertime. She looked rested, freshly showered and happy. She kissed me on the cheek and said, "Any sign of that mystery boy?"

I shrugged, wishing I'd never mentioned Goth. "I've been sleeping. I only just woke up."

"Me too. I slept for almost four hours. The best sleep I've had in more than a year. Did they feed you dinner?"

"I guess not."

"You guess not? That means no." I thought she'd jump up and run out to the nurse to demand my dinner. But she didn't. Instead, she reached into her purse and brought out a napkin-wrapped piece of cheesecake. My favorite dessert. "I went to this charming little place for dinner. All the places around here are charming. It's really a very pretty area. Old Mrs. Trumbull, the woman who runs the B&B, told me there's an ordinance against chain stores. The nearest Walmart is thirty miles away. Doesn't that sound lovely?"

I wasn't sure if it was lovely or not. My mom hated Walmart so much, I'd never actually been. When she talked about it, it sounded terrible. But I knew not everything my mom hated was all that bad. I took the cheesecake and looked at it. I sort of wanted it. It was cheesecake, after all. But the idea of breaking off a piece and eating it didn't appeal to me. In fact, it kind of made my stomach turn.

"I probably won't have it until later. I'm not all that hungry," I said, putting it on the nightstand.

"Did you see the doctor?" My mother asked, finally getting down to business.

"He came and examined me. He seemed concerned about my circulation."

"As he should be. If your heart's not beating, you're not alive."

She was right. So, I guess it wasn't too weird. Then she asked, "Do you think he's related to Debbie Harry?"

"Blondie?" Classic rock was her thing not mine. Which didn't stop her from acting like I should know everything about it.

"Of course, Blondie. Wouldn't it be funny if he was like her brother or something?"

"Yeah, I'm sure the doctor is related to a famous rock star." Although it wouldn't be the weirdest thing that had happened in the last few days.

"New wave, Jake. It's different."

I knew it was different. She'd told me a hundred times. "Whatever."

"I called your father. He sounded dubious."

"Well, he would. I wanted him to convince you to let me go, to let me die. Your calling him up and telling him I'm going to live the very next day, that *would* sound suspicious."

"You mean he thinks I'm crazy?"

I bit my tongue. Of course he thought she was crazy. They were divorced. That's what divorced people thought about each other.

"Well, that explains a lot," she sighed. "He insisted I have you Skype with him. I tried to explain about the reception problems here, but that just made him more suspicious. I mean, really, it's like he thinks I've kidnapped you, and he wants proof of life before sending the ransom. I'll have to ask to see if they get reception anywhere in the building. I always knew you'd be okay, Jake. Always. But lately, I began to think maybe it was just wishful thinking, that I might have been fooling myself. I wasn't, though. We found a way through."

Tears streamed over her smiling cheeks. I really wanted to avoid the whole emotion thing. Especially since I wasn't quite as convinced everything was going to be okay. I mean, I was still lying there with tubes running in and out of me, right? Couldn't she see that? This might have been part of why I was kind of annoyed with her. She was so sure everything was suddenly okay. I mean, holy shit, if I up and died, she was going to be a mess.

I mumbled, "It's okay, Mom" and "Everything's going to be fine." I waited, desperate to change the subject but needing her to calm down before I did it. Finally, she wiped the tears off her cheeks and gave a little laugh at how silly she was.

"Dr. Harry won't tell me how long I have to be here," I said, lowering my voice as though I might wake the men across the room. Or worse, make them jealous because I could think about leaving while they probably couldn't even think.

"All of this is very new, Jake. I imagine they're going to want to study you for at least a little while. We might even have to come back. It doesn't matter, though, does it? As long as you're getting better."

"Mom, how much is this place costing? Can we afford this?" It was hardly what you'd call fancy, but that didn't mean they wouldn't be charging an arm and a leg. Especially if I was having daily tests.

"It's research, sweetie. It's not costing us anything."

"Not even our insurance?"

"Insurance doesn't cover things like this."

"So, everyone who comes here is being researched?"

"I would think so, yes."

I nodded toward the two elderly men across the way. "Do you think they're in the study?"

My mom looked over at the comatose men. After giving me a mischievous look, she scampered across the room. I hissed, "Mom. What are you doing?"

And then she began to talk to them. "Hello. I'm Cheryl Rogers-Margate, and I'm here with my son, Jake, who had leukemia. He's had his first treatment and we're very hopeful. We're so impressed with Dr. Harry. I hope he's doing wonderful things for you..." She glanced at a clipboard hung on a hook to the bottom of the bed. "A. Cummings and you... C. Ridley. It's very nice to meet both of you, by the way."

She paused as though she might get a response.

"Well, I hope you both have a pleasant day. I'll come by and say hello another time." She walked back to me and whispered, "They say it's good to talk to people when they're unconscious like that."

I whispered back, "Is it good to mock them? Because that's what you were doing." I couldn't believe it. My mother had managed to mortify me in front of the unconscious.

"Jake! I was not mocking anyone."

"Yeah, I'm sure they appreciated your little chat," I said, with definite snark. Then I had a truly unpleasant thought. "I hope that's not what Property Five does to you." It would suck to live but have my life fast-forwarded at the same time.

"Don't be ridiculous," my mom said. "They're obviously here for another reason. It's a research institute. I'm sure they're researching all sorts of things."

"Yeah, this place is hopping."

"Jake—"

"Well, come on, it doesn't seem like an institute. Dr. Harry said the place was his, like he'd paid for it all. Why would—"

"I don't pretend to understand the things rich people do." That was a line she'd used before to dig at my dad.

"Rich people put their names on things. They don't run—"

"Jake—"

"It seems more like the kind of place a mad scien—"

She burst out laughing. "Oh my God! Next you'll tell me you met Igor and the Bride of—"

"I'm just saying."

"You need to work on your attitude. Don't be such a naysayer."

"I don't know what a naysayer is," I said, though I knew exactly what it was. It's kind of obvious. Nay. Sayer. And I didn't think my attitude was the problem. *Her* attitude on the other hand—

"Jake, you know perfectly well those men aren't here for the same reason you are. When you do a scientific study, the participants have things in common. They're here for another study, I'm sure." She smiled at me stiffly. I wasn't sure she believed what she'd just said. I mean, what study were they here for? The health benefits of being unconscious for an extended period?

Standing up, she asked, "Where is the restroom? I've had a lot of coffee this afternoon." She watched my face for an answer. But I had no idea where the restroom was. I'd been in bed all day. That seemed to dawn on her. "You don't know, do you? Of course, you don't. They've been bringing you bedpans all day."

"No. No, they haven't."

Her mood changed. "They haven't? What do you mean they haven't? Jake, when was the last time you peed?"

"I don't know. Before we got here."

"That's not good. That's really not good," she said and hurried out of the ward.

thirteen

The ward was dark but for the light coming from the machines monitoring my two ancient roomies. I sat up in bed to look out the window but could barely see anything besides dark, skulking trees and a faint light in the distance. A neighbor? A buoy out on the lake? I swung my legs over the edge of the bed, then stood. It seemed like a long time since I'd stood. It felt wobbly, unstable. Carefully, I walked out into the aisle between the beds.

The rest of The Godwin Institute was out there. I wanted to see what my mom had told me about. What was it really like? I was quickly at the door to the ward, through the wide arch. To my right was the reception desk, Miss Haggerty slumped over in her chair, snoring. To my left, a hallway slipped behind the stairs.

As quietly as possible, I turned that way. At the end of the hallway was the solarium, a good-sized room with windows on three sides and a windowed door on the far wall. The windows were wooden, original.

You didn't see that in Chicago. Wooden windows. Windows in Chicago were always metal. Aluminum, I think. Better for insulation. These old wooden windows let in drafts and had hooks that loosely fit into eyes on each side.

There was a matching summer sofa and two rattan chairs. The cushions were done in a tropical pattern. Palm trees and parrots. A coordinating coffee table sat between them, with a card table in one corner. I imagined myself playing rummy with the old men in my ward. They remained comatose in my imagination, slumped across from me forever unable to play their cards.

On the far side of the solarium was another door leading to a hallway on the other side of the stairs. I was about to walk over and investigate, but something caught my attention.

Outside, the yard was bathed in moonlight and nearly as bright as day. A girl stood by a tree about twenty feet from me. She was around twelve, standing very still. Even the trees moved more in the wind. She looked sick. Emaciated. Almost skeletal. And at the same time, I could see she'd been a pretty girl. Blond hair. Button nose. Happy once. And while I was thinking that she opened her eyes.

They were milky and opaque and terribly afraid.

fourteen

"Psst."

I struggled to open my eyes.

"Psst."

And then I did open them. Goth sat next to my bed holding a cheap smartphone, its light casting an eerie glow on his face that made his eyes seem darker and his skin paler.

"Does that work?" I asked.

"No. There's no reception here. It's just a very expensive flashlight."

"Bummer."

I glanced over at the reception desk. Miss Haggerty was slumped over, snoring. That was weird. She'd been doing that in my, my what? My dream? Had that been a dream? It didn't feel like—

Cigarette smoke. I smelled cigarette smoke. Miss Haggerty had smelled like smoke the night before. But I couldn't be smelling—

"I smell cigarette smoke," I said.

"Yeah, I just went out and had a cigarette. Sorry, I hope it's not too disgusting."

Using the remote, I sat the bed up all the while watching the spark in Goth's eyes. "Lemme guess," I said. "Lung cancer?"

"Lung cancer would be an improvement. Cystic fibrosis."

"Oh. I thought they were researching cancer here." Had anyone actually said that? I couldn't remember.

"So, you had cancer?"

"Leukemia. I mean, I still—" Did I still have leukemia? I wasn't even sure.

Goth started to say something and coughed instead. He put a fist in front of his mouth and coughed again, hard and heavy. His lips were bluish, even more so than his skin. He saw me staring and smiled when the coughing stopped. His teeth were really, really nice.

"Are your mom and dad here?" I asked. "My mom's staying at a B&B."

"No, they're not here. I've got five brothers and sisters. All younger."

"That's a big family."

"Two of my brothers have CF."

"Wow."

"Yeah. There's only a twenty-five percent chance of passing the disease. But my parents got three out of six."

"I guess they shouldn't go to Vegas with that kind of luck."

That made him laugh. Which made me laugh. Then I realized it wasn't all that funny. "Your parents are at home taking care of your younger brothers?"

"Basically."

"You miss them?"

He looked me over, shrugged, and said, "They didn't want me to come here. They wanted me to die at home. But I wasn't into it."

"I have brothers and sisters. Well, no full siblings. Just halflings and steplings." He didn't say anything. "I thought people with CF lived longer than they used to."

"That's the other thing. My parents aren't big on doctors. I had to get a lawyer when I was fourteen so I could get treatment. That pissed them off. The lawyer represents my brothers now. That pisses them off more. They'd never say it, but they're glad to see the last of me."

"My mom is the opposite of your parents. I can barely give a urine sample without her standing over me."

He chuckled, then coughed a few times. I couldn't believe the things he'd done. The way he'd fought back against his own parents. It barely occurred to me to disagree with my mom no less get a lawyer. I mean, his parents definitely sounded awful, but I did get the impression that Goth would stand up to anyone. He wasn't really Goliath, he was David.

"What are you going to be when you grow up?" Goth asked.

I shrugged. "Up until two days ago, I wasn't planning to grow up."

"Yeah, it's hard to plan on a PhD if the program is longer than the rest of your life. But, hey, now you can get a PhD. You could get two."

That was an overwhelming thought. I could choose. I had time to make choices. Wow, that was different. I shrugged it off, saying, "Um, at the moment I'd settle for getting out of bed."

Goth leaned in close, like there were people around he didn't want to hear his next question. "So, are you?"

"Am I what?"

"Are you gay?"

I didn't know why he asked me that. Was he gay too? Or was he deciding if he should avoid me. "Um, I guess."

"You guess? You mean you're not sure?"

"I've been sick so long I didn't think I'd get to be anything."

"Well don't worry, I'm gay too."

"Oh. Cool."

That felt weird and interesting and frightening all at once. Goth had kept talking and I hadn't heard him, so I said, "What?"

"I said, that's another thing with my parents. They don't like that I'm queer. Or that I want to stay alive. They don't say it, but they think it's God's will to smite me."

I think he was trying to be funny, but he seemed messed up about his parents. I wanted to say something that would make it a little bit better but all I could come up with was, "That sucks."

"Big time." He rolled his eyes and stood up.

"When do you start your treatment?" I asked.

"Not for a week or two. Dr. Harry said he's waiting for some results, and if they're as good as he hopes, he'll start my treatment."

The thing that popped into my head right away was that the results he was waiting for were mine. If my results are good, Goth would start his treatment.

fifteen

Ping. Ping. Ping. I woke to the pinging sound of kamikaze flies throwing themselves against the screen that covered the open window next to my bed. There were half a dozen of them, and every so often one would fly away and then dive bomb the screen as though it might somehow fly through it. They seemed to be taking turns, hoping if they hit the same spot over and over, they'd break through. But that was stupid. Flies weren't organized—that was my sleep-numbed mind talking.

Slowly, I became aware the bed was damp and cold. I'd wet myself. It was good I'd begun to pee again. It was not good I'd done it while I was fast asleep. The night before, my mom had gone out to talk to the nurse about my woeful lack of urinary output. A few minutes later, she'd come back and said, "Miss Haggerty called Doctor Harry. He said it's nothing to worry about." She tried to smile but didn't do so well. Our old doctors would have freaked if I didn't pee at exactly the right time in exactly the right amount.

I poked around until I found the buzzer down around my hip and rang it. Nurse Margie hurried through the arch into the ward. "I, um," I tried to think of what the medical way of saying I pissed the bed was exactly. Finally I went with, "I soiled the bed." I cringed when I said it. It sounded like I'd just rubbed dirt all over the bed, which was almost worse than what had really happened.

The whole time Nurse Margie was changing the sheets, I thought about the dream I'd had. It had seemed real, though I knew it couldn't be. It was like the other dreams, but then it wasn't. I hadn't been floating up near the ceiling. I'd been walking around. It was freaky, though. That shouldn't have been surprising. The whole institute was freaky and weird and vaguely disturbing. Having weird dreams was a pretty reasonable response, I guess.

Of course, it was a dream. The furniture in the solarium told me that. Palm trees and parrots? In the Midwest? No, I'd been dreaming. And that little girl. It was highly unlikely a twelve-year old girl was wandering around the backyard.

I've seen too many horror movies, I told myself. *Yeah, that's it.* That had to be it. Everything here was normal and I was just, like, imagining things. I believed that for almost an entire minute. No, this place was weird and weird things were happening around me. For example, the two old men across from me who seemed to be—well, if they weren't dying, they certainly weren't living.

And what about Goth's midnight visit? That wasn't a dream. We'd really come out to each other, right? It was weird we were both gay. Had Dr. Harry figured that out somehow? Was he trying to save young gay men? Or was there some genetic component that made Property Five work better on us?

While we were changing my pajamas, Nurse Margie said, "When we're done, I'll draw blood for the day. Then you're scheduled to go upstairs for an EEG and a PET scan."

"How will I get there?"

She looked at me like I was mentally unstable. "You're going to walk."

Other than in my nightmare, I hadn't taken a step in about thirty-six hours. Or was it forty-eight? Not that being dragged in from the car when we arrived really counted.

"So, it'll be like a field trip?"

"I don't know if I'd go that far. It's just upstairs. We took my son's sixth grade class canoeing on Duck Lake. *That* was a field trip. One of the teachers got it in her head it would be a good idea to walk the kids up the Meehawnee Trail. Seven miles. With sixth graders. I mean, I know the kids are all overweight, but one seven-mile walk isn't going to fix that, now is it? Plus half of them kept sneaking off to smoke. And I don't mean cigarettes.

Sixth graders! I was shocked. Of course, *you* know what kids are like. You practically are one."

She pulled the blanket back up over me now that everything was clean and dry. Then she opened up my pajama top and began checking the dressing covering the spot where my Hickman had been.

"I *am* sorry," I said.

"About what?" she asked, pulling on the tape that held down the bandage. Never fun.

"Peeing the bed."

She got all the tape off and lifted the gauze off the Hickman scar, looked at it, and said to herself, "Huh, no blood." To me she said, "You couldn't help peeing the bed. No one needs to be sorry about things they can't help. That's what I tell my son. He peed the bed until he was nearly twelve. Couldn't help it. Hormonal, the doctor said. Though my ex-husband was sure it was all psychological."

She smiled at me nervously, seeming to remember my problems weren't hormonal or psychological and it was still possible I might not be growing out of them. She deftly put a new piece of gauze over the Hickman scar and, unfortunately, taped it down again.

"That's the thing about kids today," she said. "One minute they're peeing the bed, and the next they're off sneaking joints in the woods." Then she walked out of the ward.

Wait a minute. In a weird way, I *would* be growing out of my problems. Maybe I already had. I wasn't going to die of acute blah-blah-blah leukemia. I was going to live. Just thinking about it felt weird. I didn't miss being on the verge of dying. Not exactly. But I didn't really remember any other way to live.

And what did that mean exactly? To live? I was now faced with a question I hadn't been able to ask myself for years. What was I going to do when I grew up? Did I want to go to college? Did I want to get a job? What was I good at? I was a good patient, but no one paid you for that. And what about living on my own? Did I want to? Did I want to find a boyfriend? Or did I want to find a lot of boyfriends? I'd come to terms with dying, and that had been hard. Now I had to come to terms with living. I hoped it wasn't going to be as difficult. Though at that precise moment, I wasn't sure. It was kind of like having to take a test in English class and realizing I hadn't shown up for months, so I had no idea what the answers were supposed to be.

Nurse Margie was back with an empty pint-sized plastic bag and a new IV set-up. She gave me a sweet smile as though she was bringing me candy and said, "I'm going to move the line up further, and then we'll take your blood."

"You're going to fill that whole bag?"

"It *is* a lot, isn't it?"

"Are they raising vampire bats in the attic?"

"Hard to say. Things *are* pretty secretive around here. I do know you're going to be getting a special treatment every afternoon while you're here. And that Dr. Harry is very happy with your progress so far. You certainly look better than you did yesterday." She smiled at me, then pulled the old IV out of my hand, pressing a ball of cotton onto the tiny hole. "Hold this."

I pressed down on the ball while she wrapped an elastic band around my bicep and began looking for a new vein without much success. "You've had a lot of chemo, haven't you?"

I nodded.

"Not so good for the veins." She stuck me a few more times until she finally got a vein just below my elbow. With a sigh, she relaxed. Really, she'd been tenser about it than I'd been. It hurt but not as much as I'd have thought. Not as much as it used to. She began to fill the bag, taking a whole pint of blood from me.

"This is the only time we'll have to do this, right?"

"No, this is part of the treatment. It's on the schedule each morning," she said, unable to look at me.

An entire pint of blood each morning? That worried me, it worried me a lot. I was too sick to make that much blood. Wasn't I? I tried to think about how many pints of blood I had total. Eight? Nine? If they took a pint every day and I had trouble replenishing the stock, how long until I was running on empty?

"That seems like a lot of blood."

"You'll be getting the same amount put back in. That's the afternoon treatment."

So they're taking my blood out and putting it back in. What happened to it in between? I decided not to ask her.

"When will I see Dr. Harry?"

"I believe he's at a conference for the next few days. He'll be looking at your results every day, though. Via email."

"So there *is* wi-fi here?"

"Only DSL. In Dr. Harry's office. Part of the whole secrecy thing." Then she lowered her voice, "All the employees have to sign a non-disclosure agreement. Seems kind of extreme, if you ask me. Not to mention I keep violating it left and right." She looked at the pint bag filling with my blood. It wasn't filling quickly. She got a quizzical look, then reached out for my free arm and took my pulse.

"What's the matter?"

"Your pulse is a bit low, that's all. I'll put that in the email later today."

It all seemed kind of weird. I mean, there were four of us at the institute, well, four that I knew of. Two of us were in a coma. And Dr. Harry went to a conference? Shouldn't there be another doctor?

"Dr. Harry is the only doctor here? Isn't that weird?"

"I've never worked research before. It's probably completely normal." She sat down on the bed next to me, and we waited while I slowly bled into a bag.

"How long have you been a nurse?"

"Nearly ten years. I started out at a regional hospital. Was there nearly five years, but then...well, office politics. You're too young to really know about that, but it can be vicious. I was off for a while after that. Just as well. I got to spend time with my son, not that he appreciated it. Then I was at Glen Lake Urgent Care for a year. Maybe less. And now I'm here."

She hopped off the bed and checked the bag of blood, decided it had filled enough and unhooked me. Then she positioned herself next to the bed. "All right, let's get you upstairs."

I swung my legs over the edge of the bed just as I had in my dream. I stood up and looked across the room. The old men were gone. Their beds were empty. They'd been taken away while I was asleep.

"Hey, where—"

And then I passed out, landing on the floor with what I can only guess was a loud squishy thud. When I came to, Nurse Margie was pushing the last of me back onto the bed. I was face down, ass in the air, feet dangling. Nurse Margie was sweating. She must have struggled to get me onto the bed all by herself. Seeing my eyes open, she said, "You went out like a light."

"Did that happen because my blood pressure is low?"

"I couldn't say. Maybe."

"But you'll tell Dr. Harry about it?" I asked.

"Yes, of course."

"Where'd they go?"

"Where'd who go?"

Nodding my head toward the other side of the room. "The old men."

"Oh, them. I heard someone say Dr. Harry moved them to an extended care facility downstate."

"He couldn't make them better?"

"I imagine they'll be more comfortable." Then she considered saying something she seemed to know she shouldn't. "I've been here three months. You're the first success story I've seen."

What did that mean? It felt like a huge responsibility. Being first. The idea of it made me tired, very tired. Without intending to, I drifted off to sleep.

sixteen

The next day, my mother was there when Nurse Margie came to take my vitals. Dr. Harry must have thought my low blood pressure and passing out like a drunk at the end of a three-day bender were just fine because nothing was said or done. After I bled out another pint, Nurse Margie unhooked me from the IV, and then she and my mom slowly got me up and acclimated. Despite a dizzy wave or two, I managed to remain conscious.

Yay me. I was racking up the accomplishments left and right.

We paused on the landing. I needed to catch my breath. That gave me time to take a close look at the resurrected Jesus. We hadn't seen each other since the night I arrived. The two of us, me and the savior made of glass, were almost the same size. I noticed he didn't look as gray as he did the night I got there. Light coming through the window turned his skin almost yellow, making him jaundiced, as though his resurrection wasn't going well. And, hey, maybe it wasn't.

There's nothing to say that things hadn't been a little bumpy between being resurrected and lifted up into heaven to enter the family business. I mean, seriously, even if someone had originally, truthfully written down in the Bible, "Jesus was brought back to life except for a bad case of liver damage," someone else would have come along and erased it. Nobody wanted an imperfect messiah.

That reminded me, although don't ask me why, of my former room-mates. I asked my mom, "The old men are gone. Did you see that?"

"Of course, I saw that. Concentrate on what you're doing."

"You didn't say anything."

"I thought they might have, you know, passed."

"Nurse Margie says they went to a home downstate."

"That's what Dr. Harry told me," Nurse Margie added. That was weird. Before she'd said "someone" told her. Now that someone was Dr. Harry. I wondered if Nurse Margie had a problem with the truth. She certainly had a problem keeping her mouth shut.

"Well, that's good. It's better than passing."

"So, does that mean Dr. Harry is back from his conference?"

Nurse Margie shrugged underneath my arm. "I haven't seen him."

"But he must be back if he sent the old men to a nursing home."

"Maybe. There was a note on the nurses' station. That's all I know."

A note? Totally bizarre. "Someone" had told her what happened to the old men. Dr. Harry had told her what happened. And now it was a note. I wondered if she had any idea at all what happened to the old men.

When we reached the second floor, I made them stop. I felt weak, like my energy had dribbled out of me as we climbed the stairs. I wanted to lie down on the dusty wooden floor and sleep forever. Except I couldn't. My mom and Nurse Margie held me up. I looked down the hallway that sliced the second floor into two halves. Doors were cut into each side, maybe five, I don't know. I wasn't in a counting mood. Everything was painted putty like the downstairs, a dull, lifeless color that made me think whoever chose it got bored partway through deciding and just said, "That one." Putty was the color of giving up. Which at that moment I wanted—

"It's this way," Nurse Margie said, pulling me to the left.

Had these been classrooms when the building had been a boys' school? Or had they been dormitories? What was it like to go to a boys' school? Maybe the place was haunted. Little boys caned to death by—

We stopped, and Nurse Margie opened one of the doors. We walked into what seemed like an office. There was a built-in desk against one wall, with two computers sitting on it. Over the desk was a window that looked into the room next to us at a machine shaped like a giant metal donut. I'd done this before, so there weren't going to be any surprises. I was about to be laid on a too-narrow table and repeatedly slid back and forth through a metal donut hole, a process that would have been more enjoyable if there were actual donuts involved. Except I didn't want a donut. Why didn't I want a donut?

Sitting at the desk, was a tall, unwieldy guy with dark hair and a bad attitude. "This is Ray," Nurse Margie said. "Ray, this is Jake Margate. You'll be seeing a lot of Jake."

His eyes were algae green, bloodshot, and a bit crossed. There was something reptilian about him. If you told me his blood was colder than mine, I would have believed you. He looked me over and decided he was unimpressed. He was only a few years older than me and still had fresh acne scars on his cheeks.

After mumbling a sort of hello, he led us into the room with the machine. He and Nurse Margie helped me lie down on the thin metal table. Then he covered me with a thin blanket. I was uncomfortable, but at least I was lying down.

He hooked me up to another IV, and something bright red began to flow into my veins. Oh my God, I realized I'd gotten my wish. Colored chemo! Shit, Ray was asking me something.

"What?"

"I said, did you take everything out of your pockets?"

"I don't have anything in my pockets." I still wore *The Simpson's* pajamas. Did he really think I'd shove my keys and some change into my pockets to hang around all day in bed?

"You're not wearing a belt, are you?"

"No. Not with pajamas."

I had the uncomfortable feeling a manual somewhere told him to ask these questions. I looked at my mother and used what energy I had to roll my eyes. She pursed her lips at me the way she always did when I had an opinion that didn't match hers.

Ray left the room. Nurse Margie and my mom stood there a moment, and then Nurse Margie said, "I think we're supposed to leave, too. You know, radiation."

"Of course," my mom said. It wasn't her first time at the rodeo.

The two of them walked out and closed a thick door behind them. That left me alone in the room with the metal donut. Having done this before, or at least something similar, I knew Ray would talk to me through an intercom system. He'd push a button and slide me into the machine and tell me when to hold my breath. The donut would make a whirring sound kind of like a small turbine engine. Then I'd slide out again, and Ray would tell me to breathe.

Except that isn't how it went.

Nothing happened for a long time. I just lay there. Then I heard Nurse Margie through the intercom, "I think it's this button here."

Followed by Ray. "Can you hear me, Jack?"

"It's Jake." That was my mom.

"Yeah, I can hear you." I'd been called Jack enough times not to give a shit.

"Um, good."

I waited. Nothing happened. "Are we going to start soon?"

The intercom clicked on. "Um. We have to wait a half hour after we start the IV. You have like sixteen more minutes."

"Oh. Okay."

I thought this was like tests I'd had before. But it wasn't. I was pretty familiar with the kinds of tests out there. I'd had simple X-rays, CT scans, CT scans with dye, and MRIs. This was different. This was a PET scan. Dr. Harry had mentioned it, and so had Nurse Margie. I'd heard of them before. I thought I'd even had one, but I must not have. I'd have remembered having to cool my heels for half an hour before we could even start the test.

For a moment, I wondered why we weren't doing a simple CT scan. I mean, that's what the machine looked like it was. It could do both, couldn't it? So why not do that kind of scan? The answer came to me almost immediately. A CT scan told you where there was cancer. If I was cured, there would be nothing to see. But did we know that for sure? Didn't we need a CT scan just to find out that we didn't need to do a CT scan? And what was a PET scan anyway? What did it tell you?

SEVENTEEN

"—reports of the subject's condition continue to be positive. Vitals remain on the low side but have increased. All organ systems appear to have begun functioning. Kidney function has returned. We were unable to measure first output as patient was incontinent during the night. Circulation remains suppressed, particularly in the extremities, but I'm hopeful it will improve."

Dr. Harry sat at his desk talking into his phone again. A duffle bag crammed with some clothes sat next to the desk. He'd poured himself a half glass of some kind of brown liquor. He looked stressed but not distressed, a man who had important things to do, a man who was anxious to get to them.

"It has been difficult to keep my emotions to myself. The joy I feel at my success is nearly impossible to describe. I've sacrificed so much for this. I could have had a more prominent, lucrative career if I hadn't pursued Property Five. I could have found some shred of happiness in that, however brief. But I chose not to. And now I'm glad. There were times I wondered if I was squandering my life on research that would go nowhere, could go nowhere. I hesitate to think what would have happened to me if I hadn't succeeded—no, no, I know what would have happened. I would have continued until I did succeed or until I simply died."

He took a sip of his drink, set it down, closed his eyes, and thought. About what? Was he thinking I was a real person and not just an experiment? I *doubted that. I was little more than my measurements. I was my pulse, my blood pressure, my respiration rate.*

"And then I think even if I had never succeeded, it would have been worth it because I'd tried. That was the only important thing, to try. That's wrong, though. That's the justification of someone who has failed, someone comfortable in failure. And I no longer have to justify anything. My worth has been established. Or it will be when I reach the point where I can publish my findings.

"I can't help but imagine how people will react to the news stories. The interviews. The television appearances. I've thwarted death. Most people will be grateful. Some, I suppose, will suggest I've somehow destroyed their religious faith. That if I'm able to use science to reign in death, to provide in some small portion exactly what they promise in their Bible, that somehow makes everything they believe false."

The Dr. Harry in my dream had a funny way of saying things. He'd cured leukemia, and that was a big deal. Why did he have to try and make it an even bigger deal by saying things like "reign in death?" What did that even mean? Had he cured other diseases? Did he expect to?

"Others may question the wisdom of extended life. How will the world support the human race if we can conquer all illness, all death? Yet, I wonder. If we can find a way to ward off what was once inevitable, then might we not also find solutions for things as simple as over-crowding?

"And, of course, there may be ethical—"

eighteen

Suddenly, the machine came on, waking me with its whirring noise and an unexpected jolt to the table I lay on. It began to slide into the donut. This wasn't exactly right.

"Should I hold my breath?" I asked.

"Hold your breath."

I took a deep breath and held it as I continued my slow journey into the machine. There was something space-age about the sound of the machine, and I had the random thought that my entrance into it should have been preceded by a countdown. Ten. Nine. Eight. Seven. I needed to settle in and think about something. Or nothing.

Then I was thinking about the dream I'd just woken from. Why did I keep dreaming about Dr. Harry like that? Why was my mind making up things I couldn't possibly know? I knew almost nothing about Dr. Harry's research, and I knew even less about him as a person. Why did I think I knew? I'd only seen him what, twice? Three times? He seemed mysterious. No, not seemed, was. He was mysterious. I didn't know anything about him. So, exactly what *did* I know?

I tried to figure out what year it would have been when he got out of medical school. He looked like he was in his sixties so he must have gotten out of medical school in the late seventies or early eighties. Where did he go to school? It could have been anywhere, but I decided it was Chicago.

Mainly because I knew Chicago. And they had good medical schools. I was the one inventing him, so he definitely wasn't going to some crap school in the Caribbean. Northwestern was a good medical school. I was pretty sure. Loyola, too.

I imagined Dr. Harry living in Chicago—not the Chicago I knew, but more the Chicago of *ER* reruns, the shabby, dark, always-under-construction-Chicago. I pictured him working in a big public hospital where he'd lose so many patients to cancer that the only way to recover from his sadness was to find a cure. And now he had. He'd found a cure to cancer.

It was hard to imagine he'd done something so amazing because he was so stoic. A normal person would be bouncing all over the room screaming, "I cured cancer." A normal person would be calling up *The Today Show* and demanding someone smarter than Kathie Lee Gifford interview him —though she could sit in the background gasping and mouthing wide-eyed surprise while pretending not to be drunk at ten in the morning. But Dr. Harry didn't seem like a normal person. He was more animated in my dreams. Maybe that's why I dreamed him that way, because in real life he barely reacted.

"Okay, you can breathe now," Ray said through the intercom. The machine slowed but didn't stop.

I took a breath. Something was weird, though. I didn't feel like I'd been holding my breath. Had I forgotten to hold my breath? If I'd just been in there breathing the whole time. Would Ray even notice? Would that show up on the scan?

"Take a deep breath."

It might not be exactly right to think about Dr. Harry curing cancer. He'd cured me, and I had cancer. But that didn't mean Property Five would cure everyone who had cancer, and it certainly didn't mean that it would cure every kind of cancer. In fact, certain kinds of cancer were already basically curable. Or at least almost curable.

Maybe that was why Dr. Harry wasn't jumping up and down screaming the good news at the top of his lungs. For one, he wouldn't know if it was good news for a long, long time. For two, curing cancer had kind of, sort of been done before. We just don't think of it that way. Since it could come back. Without warning.

And what about Goth? He had cystic fibrosis, which wasn't any kind of cancer. How was Dr. Harry going to cure that? Which made me wonder, was Goth even real? Or was he part of my dream?

"All right, you can breathe now," Ray said.

Oh, wow, that was stupid. The same thing happened. I must have gotten distracted and started breathing before he told me to because I didn't feel like I needed to breathe. I inhaled. It felt the same. Like I was breathing through cotton. It wasn't all that satisfying, but at the same time I didn't think about it much.

Then my mother and Nurse Margie were back in the room. Nurse Margie unhooked me from the IV. They helped me off the table. Ray hadn't come into the room with them. I could tell my mom was angry. The air around her seemed to crackle and pop.

"Is Dr. Harry aware that young man is so unskilled?" my mother asked.

"I'm sure he's properly trained," Nurse Margie said. "I can't imagine Dr. Harry would hire him if he wasn't."

"He kept looking at the manual."

I guess I was right about that.

"He was probably just brushing up. Making sure he was doing everything by the book by, you know, checking the book."

"But I don't think he *was* doing everything right. He barely gave Jake any time to breathe. I can't imagine how he got through that."

"I think I fell asleep for some of it," I said, though I wasn't sure.

"Well, that can't be good. If you were sleeping, you were breathing, and if you aren't supposed to be breathing, what will that do to the images?"

"I'll talk to Dr. Harry. I promise."

My mom couldn't say much to that. I was sure she'd talk to Dr. Harry herself, or at least try. They led me back out into the hallway. None of us looked at Ray as we made our way through the outer office. As we were about to go down the stairs, I leaned in close to my mom and said, "See, that's what happens when you don't have enough Walmarts."

"What? Jake, I don't understand. Are you feeling confused again?"

"People who should be working at Walmart get jobs somewhere else. Jobs they aren't qualified for."

She stared at me for a moment and then burst out laughing.

nineteen

The next day, I decided to see if I could find Goth. I'd gotten out of bed, after all. Not completely on my own, but still. So, after they'd taken my blood out and put it back in, I had about an hour before anything else happened. I waited for Nurse Margie to go upstairs, which she did every so often. I had the awful feeling she might be flirting with Ray, a thought which made my skin crawl a little.

I shuffled through the reception area around the stairs to the other ward only to find it empty. It was much smaller than the ward I was in. It only had four beds. The windows on one side faced out into the backyard and there was a door on the far side of the room. One of the beds was clearly occupied, though. The sheets were rumpled, and the pillows beaten into lumpy balls. A half-eaten bag of Golden Oreos sat on the nightstand next to a paperback copy of *The Sound and the Fury* and a huge box of tissues.

Standing at the foot of his bed, trying to steady myself, I looked out the windows. It was the first time I'd really done that. About a hundred and fifty feet from the main building was a dingy yellow double-wide mobile home. Well beyond that was a stand of trees, some of which were dead and stood gray and ghostly. It was the end of summer. The leaves would turn soon. Everything in front of me would die.

I mean, I suspected it was late August, but when you're ill, external events stop mattering. Seasons fade away, and the year gets portioned into weeks of chemo, weeks of recovering from chemo, two-week follow-up visits and three-month check-ups. Yeah, that all gets spread out over the same calendar a healthy person uses, but life becomes different. You stop thinking about how hot it was last summer. You think about how you spent most of it shivering under a blanket no matter how warm it got. Winter isn't about how deep the snow was, it's about the four bags of Cyclophosphamide they pumped into you over a six-week period and the mouthful of sores it left you with.

Without my illness to guide me, I would have to relearn how to tell time. Now I would notice how pretty the wildflowers were, and how nice it would be to come back next year to really see them. I'd notice the leaves when they turned, the snow when it began to fall, hoping it would stick through Christmas, the only day of the year sane people actually wished for—

Something moved outside, a tiny cloud of smoke crossing one of the windows. I went and looked out the window. By twisting my head and looking through the screen, I could see Goth standing outside smoking a cigarette.

"Hey," I said.

He didn't jump or act surprised, just looked up at me and said, "Hey. You're walking around."

"Yeah."

"That means you're feeling better."

"I guess."

"Come out here. The back door is through the kitchen."

I guessed the kitchen was through the door on the far side of the room. I went over and opened it. The kitchen was primitive, the appliances older than my mother. I slipped out the back door, down two steps, and then I was walking barefoot in the grass behind the institute.

When I got to Goth, I tried to lean against the building in the same cool way he had, but it didn't go so well. I regained my balance and just stood there, about two feet from the building watching him. He lit a new cigarette off the old one and tossed the butt out onto the lawn. Something about him reminded me of a boxer about to enter the ring. Determination? Toughness?

"I promised Dr. Harry I'd quit after he gives me Property Five," he said.

"That's not going to be easy."

"It's also not going to be that hard. I only have two packs left. I mean, I could steal cigarettes out of Nurse Haggerty's purse, but I'm too young to turn to a life of crime." He winked at me. "So, Dr. Harry is happy with your progress?"

I thought back to my vision of him telling his feelings to his cell phone. "I think he's thrilled. He feels like he beat death."

"Good. I'd like to kick the crap out of death." He smiled to cover the anger of that. "You want to walk over to the pond?"

"There's a pond?"

"Don't you hear the frogs at night?"

In all honestly, I didn't remember what I heard at night. Crickets certainly, maybe frogs, though as a city boy, I didn't really know what they sounded like.

"You think it's a good idea? Walking so far? You don't seem too well." I was definitely the pot calling the kettle black.

"Worst case scenario? I fall in and drown. Which wouldn't be that different than what's happening to me."

I wanted to tell him not to worry. Dr. Harry would save him, but that didn't even make sense. It was weird enough he could cure leukemia. He wasn't going to be able to cure leukemia *and* cystic fibrosis. I couldn't see any way that was possible. But if it wasn't possible, what was Goth doing here? I was confusing myself, so I said, "Um. Sure. Why not? Let's go look at the pond."

Surrounding the back of The Godwin Institute and the double-wide was a lot of tall grass, like a prairie almost. Goth picked out a path as though he knew right where he was going. I pushed myself to catch up to keep pace with him. My feet felt like heavy barbells. Goth was hardly moving quickly, but it was still difficult to keep up.

"What do you think of Dr. Harry?" he asked.

"He's okay."

"You think he's queer?"

"It's kind of hard to think about him having any kind of sex."

"No kidding. He'd probably take notes." Then he began a pretty good imitation of Dr. Harry's monotone. "'I understand from Nurse Margie that you're feeling aroused. The recommended treatment for that would be giving me oral sex as frequently as possible.'"

I laughed. Too much. I felt like I was betraying Dr. Harry a bit, but Goth was right. Dr. Harry probably would approach sex like an experiment. We walked over to the pond. It was about fifty feet across. The water was murky brown with occasional flashes of bright orange. Someone had filled the pond with giant goldfish.

"There's goldfish in there," I said, stating the obvious.

"Koi. They can live to be two hundred years old."

"How do you know that?"

"It's just the kind of thing I remember. I like animals and plants and shit. Those are called swamp milkweed," he said, pointing at a tall plant with a purple-pink flower. He dropped his cigarette on the ground and crushed it with a slippered foot.

"Don't you think it's weird that we're walking around out here in our pajamas?" I asked.

"Don't you think everything's weird since you got sick?"

"I guess. Yeah."

About thirty feet from the pond, near the stand of trees at what was probably the back of the property, was a vegetable garden. Goth headed over that way. The garden was made of raised, wooden boxes about a foot deep lined up in two rows of six, filled with dark, rich soil. The first boxes we came to were overgrown with weeds and vegetables gone to seed.

"Are these leftover from when this was a boy's school?" I wondered.

"I don't think so. Nurse Margie said a couple from Detroit lived here last year. They wanted to be organic farmers. I guess it didn't work out. That's asparagus," he added, pointing to a box full of four-foot-tall feathery green plants. "That's what happens when you don't pick it."

"Do you come from a family of farmers?" I asked. It felt like a strange question. I'd probably never asked anyone that before. It wasn't the kind of thing you asked people in a Chicago suburb.

"Neighbors," he said, and I had a vision of him smoking behind a sagging barn staring out at his next door neighbor's field.

The last two raised gardens had recently been turned and were nothing but boxes of deep, moist soil. "You think they're getting these ready for next year?"

"I seriously doubt Dr. Harry is growing vegetables."

I shrugged. "Somebody is,"

In my mind, Dr. Harry was weird enough to do something exactly like growing vegetables. He might even need vegetables for his experiments. For all I knew, Property Five was made of parsnips and fennel and artichokes. I stood at the foot of one of the tilled gardens and realized Goth was standing very close to me. Too close. Hovering. I gave him a questioning look.

"Where'd you go?" he asked.

"Nowhere. I was just thinking." A fly began buzzing around my head. I swatted at it.

"So, you know what? We should do it some time," he said.

I knew what he meant but I played dumb though just give myself a little time. "Do it? You mean have sex?"

"Yeah. Do *it*."

"Wow. That wasn't very romantic."

I'd given up on ever losing my virginity a long time ago—tried not to think about even—so now that I was getting an offer, it surprised me that I wasn't all that excited about losing my virginity on such a casual invitation.

"Look, we're in the middle of nowhere. You may be okay, but I might not last the week. *Carpe diem* and all that. You know?" He smiled at me. I liked the way the blue edges of his smile turned up. And then, as if recognizing my hesitation, he said, "If things were different, I'd take you to dinner first. Maybe a movie. Get to know you. But that's not going to happen while we're here, is it?"

"I guess that makes sense." He was right. We weren't going to have anything remotely resembling a romantic date in this place. And he was kind of cute.

Well, more than kind of. Those eyes.

The fly was back. And it had a friend. I swatted at them a couple of times. "Where would we do it?" I asked, dodging a dive-bombing fly. "We can't do it in the ward."

"Maybe we can. I'm being moved in with you tomorrow. I guess they've got some girls coming in. They're going to be pretty disappointed with me and you."

I barely heard him because the two flies had turned into half a dozen. I could feel them trying to land on me, and it gave me the creeps. I waved my hands around, but they seemed unperturbed. Goth tried helping me, swatting around my head.

"I need to go inside," I said and hurried away, stumbling through the tall grass back to the main building. Goth came with me, hooking his arm in mine and the two of us stumbled and gasped across the yard. The whole way, the number of flies around me seemed to grow. I felt like I was in the middle of a swarm. I couldn't be, though. A swarm would be bigger. But still, I was being dogged by more flies than I'd ever seen at one time. Maybe country life wasn't for me.

In just a few minutes, we were back inside the kitchen. I'd managed to get in with only a few flies following me. Goth looked at me and said, "Wow, that was weird."

Something odd occurred to me. He hadn't been swatting flies. They weren't bothering him at all. They'd only bothered me.

twenty

I was still kind of freaked by the incident with the flies when my mom got there. She had a large paper cup in one hand and held it out to me as soon as she got to the bed.

"Milkshake. Drink it." As she forced the drink onto me, our fingers brushed. She got that worried look I hated and grabbed my free hand. "My God, Jake. Your hands are colder than the shake."

I pulled my hand back. "It's no big deal." I didn't know that for sure, but I certainly didn't want it to be a big deal. I'd had my share of medical big deals. I pulled the blanket tighter around me.

"I should talk to the doctor again."

"Please don't do that."

"Why not?"

"He's my doctor. I should ask him. I'll ask him next time I see him. Okay?"

She looked at me with suspicion. I had the feeling she didn't think I'd bother to ask him why I felt so cold. And, you know, maybe I wouldn't.

"Drink your milkshake." She looked unhappy but clearly didn't want to pursue the issue. "I should have brought you hot chocolate."

"I don't think they want you bringing food." I took a sip of the shake. It didn't taste like much of anything, and the texture was waxy.

Tension floated in the air, so my mother talked over it like she always did when there was tension. "There's a nature trail running behind the B&B. I took an hour walk this morning. It's a ten-mile trail. I think it runs behind the Institute. Next weekend I'm thinking of walking down to see you rather than driving. It's so restful up here. And beautiful. The wildflowers are amazing. We have to get you out to see them. I'll talk to Dr. Harry. Maybe I can take you on a field trip."

"There are wildflowers in the backyard."

"You don't want a field trip?"

"I don't feel much like it."

"Well, you can't stay in bed the rest of your life. The village is so charming. They have a tiny little movie theater, a couple of women's boutiques. Nice stuff but very pricey. Several restaurants. And a Polish bakery. I almost bought you a cherry pie."

"Thank you for not doing that."

"Well, don't think you're getting out of here without having some cherry pie. That's all I have to say. They grow cherries nearby. They put them in everything. Yesterday I saw cherry hot sauce for sale. Ridiculous, isn't—"

"So, you talked to Dr. Harry, and I'm going to be here a while?"

"Yes." She managed to add a layer of defiance onto the little word. "Did you ask him about that?"

I shrugged. "They want to study me. They're not going to let me go. When are you going home?"

"When I leave here. I'm all packed up and ready to go."

"Good. Call Dad and tell him I'm okay. And explain the wi-fi situation."

"I've already done that. He doesn't believe me."

"Well, call him again."

"Jake, you know how he is. He's not going to calm down until he hears from you."

"Fine. I'll ask the nurse if I can call him tomorrow. Okay?"

She took the milkshake away from me and took a sip herself. I couldn't believe it. That was a trick right out of *How to Feed an Infant*. What did she think? That I was eighteen months old, and I'd want to eat because I saw her doing it?

"All right. I think I know where I'm not wanted. I'm going." She leaned over the bed and gave me a squeeze. "I'm so happy you're getting better, and I'm going to miss you so much this week."

"I love you. I would love you a whole lot more if you didn't make me feel like I was five years old."

"Someday you'll have kids and you'll know what it's like."

After she left, I couldn't help thinking about that. Someday I'll have kids? I wasn't sure I wanted that. College, boyfriends, kids. That was all great, I guess. No, it wasn't great. It was terrifying. Somehow life was easier when all I had to do was get to the next breath.

twenty-one

The next day, Goth moved into my ward, taking the bed to my left. Our morning ritual was similar. Vital signs. Pills—Goth took almost as many as I did—breakfast, a two-hour IV drip for me, rest for Goth, drawing blood. As Nurse Margie drew my blood, I asked, "What happens to my blood? Where does it go?"

"I don't know," she said. "I just know a courier comes by every afternoon."

"For my blood?"

"I guess so. I give your blood to Ray. Ray gives something to the courier. He may get something too, I'm not sure."

"Aren't we in the middle of nowhere?"

"We are out of the way. Oh, you know what I found out? Ray is a Heartwell. I mean, his last name is Martindale, but he's a Heartwell on his mother's side."

"Why does that matter?"

"The Heartwells go back to colonial times. Their name is on every-thing. Dr. Harry might be scared to fire him," she whispered as she pulled the needle out of my arm and took the bag of blood away.

Of course, Goth's ritual was prepping him to get the treatment, and to keep his CF under control until that happened. Mine was to monitor the effects of the treatment. In between Nurse Margie's visits, Goth and I talked about all sorts of things. Books we liked—he liked a lot more than I did. I wasn't what you'd call a big reader. Movies. TV. High school. Politics very briefly, since it bored us both. Boys. Parents. Most of the movies Goth liked were way old, from the nineties and before. He liked Hitchcock. I'd heard of Hitchcock, but other than *Psycho*, I hadn't seen any of his movies.

"You saw the remake. It's not the same," Goth had said in exasperation. I'd made the mistake of saying I liked Anne Heche even though people said she was as crazy as they come.

He'd seen all of Hitchcock's films, of course, even the super old black and white ones made in England. When it came to movies, Goth had more to say about the ones he hated than the ones he liked. He hated superheroes, dystopian futures, and anything with sparkly vampires.

He must have been super broke. His cellphone was a brand I'd never heard of, and he didn't have a laptop or even an iPad. Instead he had a portable DVD player and a stack of beat-up DVDs. He said we could watch one of his movies later if I wanted. I knew I probably wouldn't like the movie much, whichever one he picked, but I loved the idea of watching it with him.

Nurse Margie brought us breakfast. There wasn't a real cook at the institute. Most of what they fed us was packaged at the grocery store. Goth usually got takeout. I had worked my way up to a plastic cup of applesauce. That morning Goth had breakfast from Mickey Ds. I wish I could say I was jealous, but it was hard enough to eat an entire plastic cup of applesauce.

"Did you make a bucket list?" Goth asked in between mouthfuls of breakfast biscuit.

"Not really," I said. "My mom was determined that I live. I didn't bother with a list since I couldn't exactly ask for help with anything on it."

"I'm putting you on my bucket list," he said. "But don't plan to stay there very long." He gave me a devilish look as he took a bite of his thick doughy biscuit.

I didn't know what to say. He was flirting with me heavily. I liked it. But I wasn't sure, didn't really know how to flirt back. I realized no one had flirted with me for the last five years. I mean, flirting with dying kids is kind of pervy. And before that, when I was healthy, I was fourteen. A kid. Flirting with a kid is even pervier. I mean, for anyone who's not fourteen. Come to think of it, no one had *ever* flirted with me.

twenty-two

When I was sick, I wished having cancer was more like it was on TV. It might not have been as bad if I'd been stuck for months on end in a cancer ward with a handful of plucky teens. A couple of them hot guys around my age—well, played by actors in their late twenties pretending to be my age but hot all the same. That would have taught me how to flirt. Between chemo sessions I could have flirted with them and possibly taken side trips to the supply closet whenever the nausea subsided.

But it wasn't like that. At the hospital, I mean hospitals, I almost never saw the same patients or nurses or even orderlies. Not that some of them weren't sexy enough to spark a dirty thought or two but I'd never see them again. And the few times I had to stay in the hospital it was only for a few days, and I wasn't exactly crushing on the other patients.

So basically, I had no clue what I was doing with Goth. I mean, all I really knew about being gay was from TV and, you know, porn, so how I got from asexual best friend to 'wow, I didn't even know that was possible' was a little fuzzy. Okay a lot fuzzy.

Anyway, the rest of that week fell into a routine. Nurse Margie woke me and took my vital signs. She gave me a cup of weak tea and a bit of broth at lunchtime, but I was still off solid food. I was peeing more often and with enough warning that I managed to ring for a bedpan. I also had a couple of BMs. Crampy, humiliating struggles, which produced a couple of dark, withered turds that smelled like a primordial swamp. Nurse Margie snatched them away, and I assumed they went upstairs for more study. Actually, I was surprised no one gave me a gold star for passing them. I thought I deserved a ribbon, at least.

Goth flirted with me. A lot. I fumbled around trying to flirt back when I could. But I was still too weak to take myself off his bucket list. That didn't stop him from climbing into bed with me one night and cuddling.

"Cuddling with a handsome man is also on my bucket list," he whispered. I found out I liked cuddling and hoped I'd get to do a lot of it. Goth was incredibly warm and that made snuggling a little like sitting around a campfire. A sexy campfire. One that I gave occasional steamy- kisses.

Every other day I spent about an hour with Ray. He got a bit more skilled at doing a PET scan, but his social skills remained subpar. One morning, I asked, "What exactly is a PET scan for?"

"I dunno," he replied sullenly. "If I knew shit like that, why I would I work here?"

I was of the opinion that if he worked at a research institute, he really ought to know shit like that but decided not to share that with him. On the day of our second scan, he started giving me another test along with the PET. I imagine I didn't get one the first time because reading two manuals would have been overwhelming.

Along with the PET scan, I was given an EEG on Mondays and Wednesdays and an EKG on Tuesdays and Thursdays. The EEG was a boring and not very pleasant test that had Ray attaching electrodes to my head making me look like an actor about to do some CGI emoting in front of a green screen. Meanwhile, the EKG was another boring and not very pleasant test where Ray attached electrodes to my chest and legs with tape. You don't have to be particularly hairy for the removal of that tape to be, well, challenging.

The EKGs checked my heart and the EEGs checked my brain. The PET scan must check everything else, I guessed. That was confirmed when my mom came in one morning that week and said, "A PET scan measures how well your organs function."

"Thanks, I was dying to know that." I waited. Saying something like that was the kind of thing my mom would always scold me for. She didn't like any reference to the possibility I might die. Even things people say all the time like, "You're killing me" or "I would just die for a whatever." But she didn't say a thing. Apparently, dying was now just like any other word.

"The wireless at the B&B is excellent," she said, obliquely explaining how she suddenly knew all about PET scans.

"Why do we need to know how my organs are functioning?"

"That should be obvious, Jake."

"No, I mean, why do we need to know on a daily basis? That seems weird. And expensive."

"I'm sure it's not that expensive."

"I bet that machine cost a million dollars. And getting it onto the second floor probably cost another mil."

"That machine did not cost a million dollars."

"Google it when you get back to the B&B."

"It doesn't matter how much the machine cost."

"Yes, it does. If I'm the only one using a million dollar machine, it matters. It matters because it's weird."

"Jake, it's not weird. This is research. Yes, it would be a lot to spend on just you, but it's not just you. Not really. It's everyone who comes after you. This research could eventually help thousands of people. Maybe millions."

Suddenly, I felt the weight of it all. What if we had actually cured acute blah-blah-blah-leukemia? What if we cured all leukemia? All cancer? Just like in my dreams. That would be pretty amazing. And totally strange.

I mean, a couple weeks ago I was this kid who was going to die without having done much of anything with his life and now, maybe I was going to be this kid who was part of driving cancer into extinction. That was like... awesome.

And hard to believe.

After the tests, Ray would help me back down the stairs. Other things were on the second floor, some kind of lab, I think, and an office or two. Everything was behind closed doors, though, so I wasn't familiar with any of it besides the scanning room and Ray's office.

The week passed slowly. When you're sick, time is a friend and an enemy. You're constantly hoping for more of it and at the same time, there are hours, days, even weeks when you'd like to crush time, skip it, forget it entirely. The waiting is interminable. Waiting for appointments to be scheduled, for nurses to frantically tell you the doctor is running behind before they hurry off to tell someone else the same thing, for test results that will tell you how much time you have or don't have.

Now that I was better, or at least *getting* better, I was struggling to figure out how to feel about time. Right now, I hated it. I had nothing to fill it with. I was killing time and feeling bad about the slaughter. It had been so precious until just recently. I should be appreciating it, feeling joyful that I'd eventually be leaving the institute and having an entire life of time to fill with amazing things, but I wasn't appreciating it. Mostly I was bored to death.

Everything had changed. I had plenty of time. Time to spare even. Maybe even more time than I wanted. And that was beginning to frighten me the most. I had no idea if time would turn out to be a friend or a foe.

twenty-three

My mother returned on Saturday. I woke up to find her staring at me. She whispered, "Who's that?"

"That's Goth."

"Really? There really is a Goth? I thought you might be, you know, hallucinating."

"You thought I was hallucinating, and you didn't say anything?"

"I thought it would go away."

"Because that's what hallucinations usually do?"

"Well, yes, it is." Then she asked, "Is he awake?"

"Goth? Are you awake?"

He didn't roll over, just grunted.

"Sorry if I woke you," my mom said. "I'm Jake's mother, Cheryl."

He grunted again. It was very rude. Given what he'd said about his parents, though, I couldn't blame him. Parents weren't necessarily his favorite thing.

"Well, um, Goth it's nice to meet you." Then to me she said, in a completely audible whisper, "I can't believe his parents named him Goliath. It's a lovely name for a Saint Bernard, but a child?"

"Mom."

Goth rolled over and sat up. "Okay, I think I like you."

"You're not fond of your name," my mother said.

"No. I don't think many people would be."

"Well, it is better than Adolph."

"Um, yeah, it is."

"Or Genghis," she suggested.

"That too."

Then she came up blank and very nearly had to concede that Goth had the third worst name of all time. Instead, she changed the subject. "You're in the study?"

"Yeah. Hopefully, they'll start the treatment soon."

"I'm sure they will," my mom said.

Just then Nurse Margie came in and started our morning routine. My mom squeezed in and gave me a hug. "All right, I'm going to go have breakfast at this little place in the village. They have the most amazing biscuits and gravy. It's huge, so I won't be able to eat it all. I'll bring the rest back, Jake."

I smiled at her, knowing full well I'd be giving it to Goth.

Two hours later, she came back with a to-go tin from the restaurant and a white plastic bag that said CVS on the outside. She set the food down on the stand between the beds and handed me the white plastic bag as subtly as she could. It didn't matter, though. Goth wasn't paying any attention. Nurse Margie was sitting on the bed slapping him on the back to dislodge his mucus.

I glanced into the bag and saw that my mom had brought me a roll-on deodorant and a bottle of designer cologne. "Are you trying to tell me something?" I asked.

Whispering, she said, "Yes. You're a little...ripe."

"I'd love to take a shower." So far, I'd only been allowed humiliating sponge baths.

She glanced at Goth trying to hack up a phlegm ball. "Come on," she said to me. "You're getting up. You need to spend more time out of bed."

"I don't know if that's okay. No one's said anything about it."

"I'm saying it." She threw back my covers and stared at me until I swung my legs over the side of the bed.

I had been spending most of my time in bed, other than an occasional trip outside to watch Goth smoke. I can't say why I'd been virtually bedridden—a seriously stupid word by the way, I mean, I wasn't being ridden by the bed. Nor was I riding the bed. Anyway, I didn't have a good reason for not getting up more than I did. I'd been curious enough about the place to dream about it, so why hadn't I spent more time wandering around?

Honestly, moving seemed to bother me, so I hadn't been doing much of it. It wasn't painful, exactly. It was more annoying. Like my body was fighting against it. It was simpler not to do it at all.

"Where are we going?" I asked, as she pulled me to a standing position.

"To the solarium. It's nice. You could use a little sunlight. You look like a vampire." She stopped and thought for a moment. "Huh? I never thought about this, but do teenage boys find vampires as much a turn on as teenage—"

"Did you talk to dad?" I asked, mostly to avoid her question.

"Yes, he got the pictures I sent." Because there was no wi-fi to Skype with, my mom had taken some pictures of me smiling and waving. Proof of life she called it. "He still doesn't believe me when I tell him you're getting better. I told him he should come up and see for himself."

"No, that's okay. He's got the halflings and the steplings to worry about. And since I'm not dying..." We were in the hallway. "Hey, did they miss you at work?"

"They did. The temp screwed everything up. If I play my cards right, I can get a raise out of the whole thing. And I'm going to need it."

"Why? You said this was paid for."

"Not for this. For college. You're going to live, Jake." She said that a lot and each time, a big smile broke out on her face. It was starting to get annoying.

"Dad will pay for it. You should spend your money on yourself."

"But I want to." She helped me down onto the sofa in the very bright solarium. "As soon as you're back on your feet, you should start college. We might be able to get you in for the spring semester. What do you want to study?"

"I haven't thought about it. I've been focused on being sick." Actually, it was too bright in there. I had to squint.

"You know what I think? You should be a doctor. You were always good at science. Remember that chemistry set I got you when you were eight? You did every single experiment in the booklet."

"That's not a reason to be a doctor." I kind of remembered the chemistry set but kind of didn't.

"Of course it is." She smiled at me real hard. "Well, think about it. You can be anything you want. You have your whole life in front of you." She slipped her arm through mine and squeezed. "This is so wonderful, Jake. I feel like there's been a rubber band tied around my heart for years, and now it's been released."

I knew I should be feeling the same, but I just wasn't. The rubber band felt like it was still wrapped tight around my heart. I wanted to tell her she shouldn't get her hopes up. I didn't feel normal yet, and it was entirely possible I never would. I was part of an experiment, and experiments sometimes went badly. In fact, if you'd ever watched a sci-fi TV show, they almost always did. I'd be lucky as long as I didn't come out of this with some annoying superpower, like having everything I touch burst into flames. But I couldn't tell her that.

"Dr. Harry hasn't told me how long you'll be here. I'm trying to see him later. Maybe he'll have more information then."

"He's back?"

"He is. And I'm going to give him a piece of my mind. I can't believe they don't have any wi-fi in this place. You'd think with cell reception this bad, they'd at least set it up so we could email. Or Skype. It's just barbaric that I have to call the landline at the nurses' desk to find out anything about you. The least they could do would be to put a phone in here."

"Oh, I know why there's no wi-fi. Nurse Margie told me. It's because everything is secret. She told me they have to sign non-disclosure agreements. They can't talk about what happens here. Kind of weird if you think about it."

"Oh, that's right. I didn't make the connection."

"What connection?"

"We signed the same agreement before we came."

"We? I don't remember signing anything."

"You were very sick, Jake. I signed it for you."

"So I can get sued if I tell people about the treatment?"

"Technically, yes. But no one ever sues over those things. I mean, if you wrote up an article for a medical journal, sure they'd sue you, but it's not anything to worry about." She gave me a sidelong glance and then decided to change the subject. "I also brought you a piece of cheesecake. It's so good."

I felt uncomfortable. The first cheesecake she'd brought had sat in the drawer to my nightstand for a couple of days before I threw it away. I hadn't told her I'd never eaten it.

"I almost didn't get it for you since you didn't say anything about the first one. You liked it, didn't you?" she asked. "I'm sure you ate the whole thing the minute I walked out of here."

Cheesecake was more than just my favorite dessert. It had become a big thing with us. During the worst of the chemo, cheesecake was often the only thing my mom could get me to eat. It was soft and kind of melted in your stomach so if it came back up...anyway, cheesecake was more than a dessert between us. I wanted to lie and say I'd eaten it, but I couldn't.

"I, uh, I'm still not big on solid food, Mom."

"But it's cheesecake. You always ate cheesecake no matter how sick you were."

I shrugged. "Maybe things are different because I'm not so sick anymore."

She looked at me a moment, and then decided that was an answer she liked. "When you come home, we're going to have to see about you making some new friends."

Wow. Segue much, Mom?

"Yeah, I'll go hangout at the Cheesecake Factory and see who I meet."

"This is a serious conversation, Jake."

That made me uncomfortable. I hated serious conversations. Friends. She wanted me to make friends. It was a completely alien concept. I'd had friends in junior high school, but they drifted away as I got sicker and sicker. I couldn't blame them and, to be honest, I hadn't been all that interested in hearing about the things they were doing. Things I'd never get to do. But I didn't think she was talking about those kinds of friends. I was fairly sure—

"How do boys meet boys these days? Do they still go to bars or is it all on the Internet?"

She'd been Googling again.

"Mom, I don't want to talk about stuff like that."

"Unless Goth is—are the two of you—?"

I kept my eyes down, not wanting to look at her. I mean, it wasn't the gay thing. I didn't think I'd want to talk to my mom about girls either. Picking at the piping on the sofa cushion, I realized something scary.

The pattern. It was palm trees and parrots. Just like in my dream. I looked up and actually took in the room. The windows were wooden with little eyehooks. A card table was in the corner. On the far side of the room, a door led to the other ward. The solarium was just as it had been in my dream. The dream I'd had more than a week before. The dream I'd had in my bed because I could barely get out of it. This was the first time I'd been in the room. So, how had I known what it looked like?

twenty-four

The dreams were real.

Or were they? I guess I might have gotten up by myself and sleep-walked, or semi-sleepwalked, so maybe I had actually been in the solarium before. That had to be it. The dreams couldn't be true. They were impossible dreams. I wondered if I should tell Dr. Harry about them. I could just imagine him making a note about into his phone, "Patient reports impossible dreams as side effect."

Late that afternoon, I had an appointment with Dr. Harry. Of course, no one had told me. No one ever told me. Nurse Margie simply came into the ward and said, "Jake, Dr. Harry will see you now" like I'd been sitting there flipping through magazines hoping he'd hurry up. Then she walked me to the examining room.

For once, my mom didn't try to come with me. I wondered if that meant she was accepting that I wanted to make my own decisions or if she was just so happy I was getting better she didn't care.

In the examining room, Nurse Margie asked me to sit on the table. Quietly, she slunk out of the room. Dr. Harry was already in the room sitting on a stool in the corner reading over my file, which in the last ten days—two weeks? Or was it just more? God, I wasn't even sure how long I'd been there. Anyway, it had grown to nearly an inch thick. I was well on my way to another four-inch-thick file.

He was taking forever to read it too. Finally, I couldn't take the silence anymore. "Do you think it will hit the bestseller list?" He didn't laugh. Instead, he turned and looked at me blandly. I had the feeling he was about to make a note in my file about inappropriate attempts at humor. Oh God, there I go again. Imaging things. I definitely wasn't telling him about the sleepwalking, or dreaming, or hallucinating, or whatever it was.

I noticed he needed a haircut. His beard was somehow more badly trimmed than before. How had he gone to a conference looking like that? Or was that the way doctors showed up at those things? Messy and unkempt. For all I knew it was a badge of honor. The messier the doctor, the better the research. They probably walked around saying to each other, "I couldn't possibly take time out to get a haircut. My research is that important."

Of course, I suppose it *was* that important. It was keeping me alive.

"Tell me how you've been feeling," he said, slipping his hand onto my neck so he could take my pulse via the carotid artery.

"Curious."

"I meant your body. How has your body been feeling?"

Stubbornly, I repeated, "Curious. Why are you giving me back my own blood?" I asked, referring to the treatments I got in the afternoon when a bag of blood, presumably my own blood, spent a good hour dripping back into me.

"If you answer my questions, maybe I'll answer yours. How have you been feeling? Physically?"

"Lethargic, I guess." That was a word doctors loved, lethargic. "I haven't wanted to get out of bed much. I sleep a lot. I'm a little stiff, sometimes. And I just, I don't know, I feel different than I felt before. Before when I didn't have leukemia, I mean. I feel different than that." I leaned in close. "Goth has cystic fibrosis. How can you be curing both leukemia and cystic fibrosis?"

"Is that it? Those are your only symptoms?"

"Sometimes it feels like I've forgotten to breathe. I'll breathe because I remember to, and then I'll try to think about the last time I was sure I took a breath and can't really…"

"Were you always conscious of your breathing?" he asked, lifting my wrist and checking the pulse there. "Before the treatment?"

"No. I don't think so."

"Jake, no one is completely conscious of their breathing. What you're describing isn't uncommon. No one thinks about breathing unless they're sick. Any other symptoms?"

Was it dangerous not to tell him about the maybe-sleepwalking? If I didn't tell him, it would probably keep happening. But if I told him, then he was very likely to do nothing except ask me lots of questions. The dreams weren't hurting me, or at least anyone but me. The questions wouldn't hurt me either, except somehow it felt like they would. But why did I think—

"Jake, any other symptoms?"

I shook my head.

"Still no appetite?" he asked. He squatted down by the floor, pushed up one leg of my pajama bottoms and checked the pulse in my ankle.

I shook my head again. He had to look up to see my answer. I added a quick, "No."

"Bowel movements?"

"That's in the file." So was how much I peed. They made me pee into a plastic jug now so they could measure it. "Can you answer my question now? Why are you taking my blood out and putting it back in?"

He stood. I worried that he was about to reach between my thighs again. I crossed my legs. Instead, he asked, "Have you masturbated since you got here?"

"What? Why are you— Why is that important? I'm here because I have leukemia not because I need Viagra."

"You don't have leukemia, Jake. Not anymore."

I was having trouble connecting with that. I knew I was going to be okay. I knew I was getting better. But I really didn't see how the leukemia could be instantly gone. It had been with me for five, maybe six years. How could it just disappear? And how could he be so sure?

"The reason I ask the question is that a sexual response is an important indicator of health. Do you have erections in the morning when you wake up?"

"I'm not answering your question unless you answer mine."

He studied me as though deciding whether I'd keep my end of the bargain. "We've taken your blood and added specially treated stem cells."

"Why? Why would you do that?"

"Stem cells take on the properties of cells around them. And then they replicate."

"My cells can't replicate?"

"You've had a lot of chemotherapy which has done damage. This will help put you right."

"No," I said.

"No what?"

"No, I don't have erections in the morning."

"Thank you." Closing my file, he tucked it under his arm and, as he walked toward the door, said, "Eventually, I'm going to need a sperm sample."

Well, that was icky.

twenty-five

"—subject continues to have little appetite, which is an indication that the digestive system has not responded to treatment as well as other systems. That may have to do with the high dose of antibiotic we're administering to deter bacterial activity. Sexual response appears to be diminished, though subject is reticent to discuss this."

Dr. Harry chuckles at this, sits back in his chair.

"Why is it that each new generation is always perceived as being more permissive, more open about things like sex, and then it never bears out? My own generation, we were hippies, we were the sexual revolution, and look at how we're perceived now—Tea Party fanatics and Fox News junkies. Perhaps it shouldn't surprise me that the boy is...what? Inhibited? The young, it seems, are never as advertised."

He finished his drink, poured himself another, picked up the smartphone and spoke into it. "But I digress. The subject did admit to not have erections in the morning, so I will interpret that as a suppressed libido. Not surprising, though. So many systems are involved in a sexual response. Very few of the subject's organ systems are working at optimal levels. Though I hope that with continued treatments—"

He stopped, pondered his words.

"I had hoped the subject would be showing a more positive response to *treatment by this point. I am still optimistic, but that optimism is tempered with caution."*

He stopped again, briefly this time.

"Note to self: Call Dr. Callabray and discuss the results of today's blood tests. Possibly increase the ratio of differentiated stem cells to pluripotent cells by ten percent. Also discuss timeline for determining success or non-success of experiment."

Sighing heavily, he set the smartphone on his desk. He looked over at the pictures on his wall. I thought he might smile again but instead his habitual frown deepened.

"I want to save him. I want to save them all."

<h1 style="text-align:center">twenty-six</h1>

After Nurse Margie picked up our breakfast trays, Goth said, "I'm feeling kind of good today. How about you?"

"I guess I'm okay."

"I wonder if it's time to work on my bucket list." Goth even winked when he said that.

"Oh, um, well, sure."

"It's going to be a very long day. I can't wait for it to get dark," he said, raising an eyebrow.

I giggled even though I kind of wished we weren't talking about it. Now I was going to be nervous the rest of the day. Or at least, that's what I expected. Things didn't turn out that way.

Just before lunch, Nurse Margie walked into the ward with a grumpy-looking kid, late teens, leaning on her. He was short, had unruly red hair and teeth too big for his mouth. With them was a girl a few years older. She looked exactly like the boy except with longer, redder hair and bigger teeth. Before he got onto the bed, she squeezed him tight and kissed him on the cheek.

"I can't stay. You'll call me, right?"

"Yeah, whatev."

"I love you."

"Uh-huh."

"Mom and Dad love you, too."

That made me wonder what were *they* like? Two toothy, high-powered executives far too important to be bothered with their son's health? A couple of unrepentant red-haired drunks who'd wandered off on a bender? Or did they even know their son was here? Could his sister have kidnapped him and brought him on her own? Kind of like my mom.

The kid rolled his eyes at his sister. Making me wonder, *Did his parents just not care?* And then she hurried out of the ward, choking back a tear.

After settling the guy into a bed across from us, Nurse Margie introduced him as Edmond Henley. We all said, "Hey."

Then she busied herself with the roving vitals stand, and we each lay awkwardly in our beds. Watching someone get their blood pressure checked didn't exactly encourage conversation. After making notes on Edmond's brand-new chart, Nurse Margie scurried out of the ward.

As soon the door closed behind her, Edmond was out of bed and crossing the room. It was a journey of about ten feet, but he was huffing and puffing by the time he got to us. He took a moment to catch his breath and then, keeping his voice low, asked, "Is there any, uh...pussy around here?"

I almost burst out laughing. The guy could barely walk across the room. What did he think he was going to do with a woman? Of course, I probably shouldn't have been thinking that. Goth and I weren't in much better shape, and we were trying to figure a way to be alone to do pretty much the same kind of things Edmond wanted a woman for.

"There's another ward on the other side of the building," Goth explained. "I was in there to start, but they moved me over here. I think they're going to put patients in there. Who was that with you? Your sister?"

"Yeah. She's annoying. Not as bad as my mom and dad but super annoying. You should have seen my parents when I said I didn't want them to bring me here. It was like the apocalypse had started or something." He chewed on that a moment, then asked, "Do you think there will be some hotties in the other ward?"

Goth smirked at him and said, "I don't know. I asked for 8x10s, but they haven't brought them by yet."

Not even remotely getting the joke, Edmond looked at him suspiciously before deciding to ignore the comment.

"I hope they're hot," he said. "The last place I was in, there weren't any babes under forty. Not that I don't like the older ladies, but I have my standards."

I could tell Goth was working up to say something snide, so I asked, "What do you have?"

"Pulmonary hypertension."

"That's high blood pressure, right?" I asked. It didn't sound so bad.

"Yeah. In my *lungs*."

"Okay."

"I need a heart-lung transplant, and they do like fifty of those a year." He pouted like a little kid. "I'm like number three hundred and sixty-five on the list."

Goth nodded. "I looked into that." By way of explanation, he added, "Cystic fibrosis."

Edmond looked at me.

"Leukemia."

"So how bad is this treatment?" he asked. "Does it hurt? Did you throw up a lot? I hate puking."

Goth looked at me intently. We hadn't talked about this.

"It's not bad," I said. "Nothing like chemo. I mean, there are a lot of tests and shit. Like daily."

"Dr. Harry said it would be a couple weeks before I could have it," Edmond said. "I thought there'd be like a whole bunch of people ahead of me."

"There's just us," I said uncomfortably. I didn't know what he was getting at. "So far."

Edmond sat down on the edge of my bed without asking. He probably didn't have enough breath. "So how many people have had this treatment?"

I shrugged. "I'm sure a lot have. It's just—"

"It's just what?" Edmond was sort of pushy. I wasn't appreciating that about him.

"I think I'm the only one *here* who's actually had it. But there were probably a whole bunch of people before I got here." I was kind of lying. I did want it to be true, though. Maybe it wasn't a terrible lie.

"No. I don't think so," Goth said. "Their website is only a couple months old."

"How do you know that?" Edmond asked. "Are you like a hacker?"

"No. My parents have a computer, but they watched everything I did. I mean they treated anything medical like it was porn. I had to use the computer at the library, but I could only get there every few weeks. One time the website wasn't there. The next time it was."

Edmond ignored the weirdness of what Goth had said and looked at me and said, "So you're the first to get the treatment."

"No, that's not, I don't think—" I wasn't the first. I knew that. Nurse Margie had said I was the only success story she'd seen. That meant there were others. Others who hadn't—

"And we have to wait to make sure nothing weird happens to you."

Now I was uncomfortable. Edmond and Goth and everyone who would come afterward were depending on me. But no, it was fine. Dr. Harry was confident I was okay and was going to stay okay. So was my mom. But were they right? They could be wrong. Was I likely to drop dead one day? Tomorrow? Next week? And if I died, would Goth? And Edmond? And the girls who might or might not already be in the other ward? I felt pressure, but it wasn't pressure I could do anything about. I sort of hated it.

"What does the treatment actually do?" Goth asked. "How does one treatment cure different diseases? That's kind of confusing."

"Tell me about it."

"So, you don't know?" Edmond asked, a little surprised.

"I'm the patient, not the doctor."

"Yeah, but you let him just put stuff into you that you don't understand?"

"I ran out of options." The three of us were quiet. We were all way too familiar with running out of options.

"I think it has something to do with differentiated stem cells." I pulled the phrase right out of my dream.

"Oh yeah. Stem cells are cool," Edmond said. I doubted he knew much about them. But they did sound cool. Or at least they'd been in the news a lot. "Was that on the website?"

Goth sat up and let his legs hang off the bed. "Sure, I think so." I had the feeling he was lying, mostly to make himself feel better, the way I had.

"So, the treatment has something to do with growing new cells?" Edmond looked at Goth then at me.

I shrugged. "I dunno."

"I can see how growing new cells would help cancer. Like for your immune system maybe," Goth pondered. "But my disease is genetic. And Edmond's is kind of structural. How would new cells help us?"

"Maybe it's about growing healthy new cells to replace your sick ones," I guessed. That would teach me to pick phrases out of random dreams.

"But we're sick in different ways."

I shrugged. "You know, my mom was the one who found this place. I was too sick to ask a lot of questions. What did it actually say on the website?"

"It was a lot of medical talk and even that didn't say much. It was like they wanted test subjects but didn't want to give much away," Goth said.

That actually made sense. It was in keeping with the whole secrecy thing.

"Dr. Harry found me. My sister made a 'Save Edmond' website. She used my baby pictures. It kind of went viral. I only agreed to do it because I thought it would get me a girlfriend or two. Instead, I ended up here."

Something began to make sense. The Godwin Institute wasn't about cancer, but it was about terminal illness. Dr. Harry had been doing something with the two old guys who'd been here and then disappeared, and the little girl, too. If there even was a little girl, I mean, I dreamed her. Right?

But if there was a little girl, she'd obviously been very, very sick. Had Dr. Harry tried to cure her and failed? Was that what happened with the old men? He'd given them Property Five and—

No, wait, there were Properties One through Four. Is that what he'd used on them? Property Four? Or Three? And now that Property Five was working, Dr. Harry had looked for subjects like me, young and terminal. He was changing the formula and the subjects. It had been a long time since I'd had a science class, but that didn't seem like good science. You weren't supposed to change more than one variable at a time.

"I did Google Dr. Harry," Edmond said. "But all I found was some stuff on life extension. Did you know there's a whole magazine about life extension? And a secret society?"

I didn't know, but it made sense. The world was full of people who wanted to live forever. My bet was that most of the stuff out there was just about being super healthy. Dr. Harry, though, had something that might really work. It was a hard thing to believe, but—weird dreams aside—I was beginning to.

twenty-seven

That afternoon, I was almost finished with my stem cell/antibiotic/and whatever else treatment when Goth said, "I'm going to go have a cigarette or two." He tipped his head in a way that meant he wanted me to come with him when I got unhooked.

Edmond stood up a little too quickly and sat right back down, "I'll go with you. And maybe we can check out the other ward." He threw in a lascivious wink. "See if any babes—"

I cringed. The whole point was to go some place Edmond wasn't.

Goth said, "Yeah, um, aren't you supposed to begin your baseline testing soon?"

"I'll just tell Nurse Margie where we're going."

"That's not a good idea. She's going to know you're going out to smoke. That will get you a ten-minute lecture. I'll be back inside before she's done."

"But I'm not having a cigarette. I'm just tagging along to see if the ladies have arrived."

"She won't believe you. But, hey, go ahead and give it a try."

Edmond obviously wanted to go but couldn't if Goth wasn't going to be with him every step of the way. He was in bad shape and knew he needed someone with him to lean on or pick him up if he face-planted. "Maybe I'll go later. The tests are important, huh?"

"Yeah, they are," I said. "Missing them would be a bad idea."

Goth shrugged and left. Edmond and I stared at each other. After a long bit, during which my IV stand beeped to indicate it was done, Edmond said, "He doesn't like me, does he?"

"I don't know. Why wouldn't he like you?"

"People don't like me."

That made me feel like shit. I didn't like him much. I doubted Goth liked him, but that didn't mean I wanted him to know it. "You just got here. He doesn't know you well enough to not like you."

He perked up. "Yeah, that's right. Maybe he'll like me later. Maybe if I give him some tips on how to attract the ladies."

"That might do it," I said. It wasn't even close to truthful, but I didn't think it was my place to explain how wrong Edmond was.

Nurse Margie came in. She unhooked me from the IV and told Edmond it was time for him to go upstairs. He had to lean on her before he was even halfway across the ward. Still, he managed to huff out the question, "Are there any nude beaches nearby?"

"Oh, how would I know that?" Nurse Margie said, as though she'd never imagined anything remotely sexual. That was clearly untrue since she'd mentioned her son several times. She'd had sex at least once.

I waited as patiently as I could for them to leave. Then I waited a bit longer. I didn't want to catch up with them as they climbed the stairs. My heart was pounding harder than it had in weeks. I would have thought it was the treatment I'd just had, but it wasn't. It was Goth. We weren't going to be able to do anything in the ward that night, but maybe we could find somewhere outside to mess around a little. Or a lot. That was the thought that had my heart going. And certain other areas tingling. I made a mental note to never tell Dr. Harry about the tingling in those other areas.

When I couldn't wait any longer, I got off the bed and shuffled out of the ward. The front desk was empty, of course. Nurse Margie was busy delivering Edmond to Ray's incapable hands. I could almost hear their conversation, Nurse Margie introducing Edmond, Ray, and Edmond grunting at each other. Or did I actually hear it somehow? I pushed the thought away. I didn't care. I slipped down the hall to the back of the building. Once I was in the solarium, I stopped and looked out the windows.

The girls had arrived, I could hear them chattering in their ward. Edmond would be thrilled. They were asking each other questions about the treatment, wondering who else was here, talking about Dr. Harry. One of the girls thought he was attractive for an older man. I thought he had *been* attractive once, but now he was just an old guy who couldn't manage to trim his beard or iron his clothes.

Edmond would freak-the-f-out. They were girls. I was pretty sure he'd like them no matter what they looked like. But would they like him? I didn't think so. I suspected he was right when he said people didn't like him.

I focused on the backyard, trying to see where Goth had gone. I didn't see him anywhere. I decided to slip out and run over behind the double wide. He might be somewhere out there.

Quietly, I slipped out of the solarium. Running through the calf-high grass, I hurried around the double-wide until I was climbing up a ramp onto a weathered wooden deck. Goth wasn't there. I searched the back of the property and didn't see him. He wasn't near the pond or the raised gardens or the woods at the back. So where was he? Had he gone into the woods?

A fly buzzed around my head. Annoying and really freaky. I wondered if something in the treatment I was getting attracted them. Like maybe I had too much glucose in my system and reeked of sugar. Knowing I couldn't stand on the deck long, I turned and studied the double wide. That's when I noticed the sliding glass door was open about six inches.

Ah, Goth must be inside.

I pushed back the screen, then the glass door and stepped inside. The place smelled musty and unused. I stood in a large kitchen with an attached dining area. An old wooden table with a couple of mismatched chairs was crowded up against the wall. The kitchen was bare, an empty space where the refrigerator should have been, with naked counters and an empty pantry next to an electric range that might be older than I was. I stepped into the living room. It was large, with nothing but an uncomfortable-looking sofa sitting in the middle of the room facing the wall. The randomness of the furniture suggested the place had been there when the Institute purchased the front building. And probably long before that.

Which made me wonder, *What were they doing with it?* Were they doing anything with it? As I walked down the hallway to the bedrooms, I discovered that yes, they were doing something with the trailer. The first bedroom I encountered was small and filled with file boxes. They were using the double-wide for storage. That made sense. Why put old files into a basement when you could put them into a nice, dry bedroom?

Then, I noticed the door to the next room. It was steel. Galvanized. The kind used for a walk-in refrigerator. It was weird, completely wrong. It didn't belong there. I'd only ever seen that kind of refrigerator in movies. I tried to remember which movie, but I drew a blank. Something scary with co-eds in a dormitory and one gets trapped inside the walk-in refrigerator. Of course, it must not have been that scary since I reached out to open the door to the refrigerated room.

But before I could get the door open, Goth spun me around and pushed me against it... kissing me. His lips were hot, deliciously hot. Is kissing always like this? I wondered. Is it always so scorching?

Oh, God, I didn't care. He was kissing me, and it was like a sunny afternoon, like being touched by the sky. He pushed his tongue into my mouth and explored. I was barely breathing, hardly wanting to breathe. His hands roamed over me, every bit as curious as his tongue. My heart jumped, paused, and then seemed not to land.

I wondered if that feeling was what love was like. Waiting for your heart to beat again. Tentatively, I rubbed my hands across his shoulders. I touched the hair on the back of his neck. I entangled my tongue with his. Doing some exploring of my own. Discovering.

And still my heart didn't beat.

Goth pushed into me, trying to get even closer. I couldn't help worrying about my heart. Behind his back, I took my left wrist into my right hand. With my thumb, I tried to subtly search for a pulse. I didn't find one. Could that be right? Could I not have a pulse? No, it couldn't be because that would mean...

I pushed Goth away. I must have had real worry on my face because he said, "Are you okay?"

"I think my heart stopped."

"Wow, that's really romantic."

"No, I think my heart stopped. Really."

twenty-eight

We hurried back to the main building. Goth huffing, his arm around me. I kept checking my wrists for a pulse and not finding one. I felt sluggish, as though I was moving in slow motion. My feet and ankles felt tighter and heavier with each step.

Goth kept giving me sidelong glances. I probably should have just said I didn't feel well and left it at that. My heart hadn't stopped. I was still standing, still walking, so it couldn't have. Why had I said something that stupid?

When we got to the nurse's desk, I said the more rational, "I'm not feeling so good."

"What's wrong?" Nurse Margie asked.

"He said his heart stopped."

"Obviously, his heart hasn't stopped." She tried not to break into a smile when she said that. She looked closely at me, expecting a practical joke or a hypochondriac, instead seeing someone very sick. "You don't look too good, though."

"I don't have a pulse."

"They're not always easy to find." She reached out a hand to take my wrist. Moving her fingers around, she searched for my pulse. She didn't find it. Kept trying. Still couldn't find it.

She told Goth to take me into the examining room. "I'm sure it's nothing to worry about." I was pretty sure she meant to comfort herself with that. She couldn't find my pulse. Of course there was something to worry about.

Goth and I went into the examining room. It looked pretty much as it had the last time I was there: neat, orderly, sterile. It was the kind of room where you should feel safe but usually felt anything but. Like a good patient, I got up on the examining table.

"I think I died the first night I was here."

"Bae, you don't seem very dead to me," Goth said.

"No, um, I..." I was tongue-tied for a moment. He called me bae. That was so...sexy. "Um, I mean, I died for a minute or two. I had this kind of vision of myself on the ceiling watching everything as it happened. And then I sort of jumped back into my body."

"So that's why you think your heart stopped? Because it has before?"

I nodded. He got a concerned look on his face then looked away for a moment and when he did he said, "Oh, man, your ankles."

I lifted them up in front of me so I could see them, pulling up my pajama bottoms at this same time; this pair was a deep blue plaid. I'd been wearing an old pair of corduroy slippers most of the time I'd been sick. My ankles and feet had turned an angry eggplant purple. That wasn't right.

My first thought was "lividity." In addition to *America's Next Top Model* and *Project Runway*, my mom and I watched all the forensic shows. I knew exactly what lividity was. It was blood pooling in a corpse after the heart has stopped. Obviously, that couldn't be what was happening to me, though it definitely looked that way.

Just then, Dr. Harry flew into the room, Nurse Margie trailing behind him. Using his stethoscope, he checked the pulse in my neck, my chest, my wrists. Without looking up, he said, "Goliath, you need to leave."

"No, that's okay, I want him to stay."

"It's not up to you. Goliath, I said leave."

He obviously didn't want to go, but he had no choice. "I'll be right outside."

"I had trouble finding his pulse," Nurse Margie said. "I'm sure it's there, it's just difficult to find."

Dr. Harry pushed me down on the table, opened my pajama top, and slipped in the stethoscope.

"What's happening to me?"

"Be quiet. I need to listen to your heart."

I did as I was told. He stepped back and studied me seriously. "Remember to breathe."

"I'm breathing."

"Not often enough. Nurse, would you get out the defibrillator?"

Fear and confusion filled her face. "But—"

"Just do it."

Nurse Margie hurried to get the defibrillator out of the cabinet. She rested it on the counter and stared at it a moment. "Doctor, you can't use this on him. He's not in cardiac arrest. Look at him—"

Dr. Harry pushed her out of the way, plugged the paddles into the machine and turned it on.

Trying to keep her voice low, Nurse Margie continued, "He's conscious. He's not showing signs of arrhythmia. Just because we can't find—"

"Step outside, nurse."

"No. You're making things—"

"OUT!"

Cowed by the volume of his voice, Nurse Margie ran out of the office. Dr. Harry set the machine and then grabbed the paddles and pressed them onto my chest.

"Isn't she right? I mean, I'm awake so I can't be having a heart—"

Dr. Harry hit a button on the paddle, and I was walloped with a bolt of electricity that felt like I'd been tackled by a three-hundred-pound linebacker—if that's actually what linebackers do, I really don't know.

Anyway, I felt like I was in a kind of shock. It hurt even after it was over, but my heart was pounding against my rib cage like it wanted to get out. I took deep, ragged breaths because they felt good, deliciously good. The unpleasant burning smell in the air may have been coming from my chest. I looked down and saw two angry red spots where I'd been shocked.

"My heart stopped. Why? And why am I conscious?"

"Your heart didn't stop. It slowed. Your pulse was barely perceptible, but it was there. You just needed a little shock to bring you back up to speed."

He was lying. Nurse Margie said you couldn't use that machine on someone who wasn't in cardiac arrest, and I had the feeling she was right.

Except she couldn't be right. If my heart had really stopped, I'd have passed out. I'd have been unconscious. And that didn't happen.

"What about my ankles?"

"Ankles?" he asked even as he moved down to them and pulled back the hems of my pajama legs. He was quiet.

"That's lividity, isn't it?"

"Lividity happens in corpses. You're not a corpse. When your heart slowed, blood collected in your feet. I assume you were standing when the episode began?" He began rubbing my ankles, helping the blood work its way back into circulation.

I didn't believe him. He was telling me parts of the truth but not all of it. So what was the truth? I was cold all the time. My body temperature ran much lower than it should. I didn't have an appetite. I felt stiff. Sometimes I forgot to breathe. I smelled bad. My heart stopped, and I didn't pass out. Blood pooled in my body. I attracted flies. An idea was beginning to form. One that made me feel numb. Number than normal.

"The night I got here, I died."

"For a few minutes, yes. But I revived you." He was still rubbing my ankles. It felt good.

"What's in it? What's in Property Five?"

He stiffened. "That's proprietary information. I can't share that with you."

"It doesn't cure leukemia, does it?"

"I saved you, Jake. Why isn't that enough?"

"I—I don't know what I am."

"You're a young man who's been sick. Very sick. And now you're getting better."

I wanted to believe him. I tried to believe him. The things I'd been feeling could be anything. Side effects. I could be experiencing side effects.

"Remember to breathe," Dr. Harry said.

"Why? Why do I need to remember to breathe?"

"Your cells require more oxygen."

"Do they?"

I exhaled as much air from my lungs as I could. Then I didn't inhale. I felt like little kid having a temper tantrum, holding my breath. Except, when I was a child and held my breath, I'd had the almost instant urge to breathe, a tugging, aching for air. The more I denied myself breath, the stronger the urge to breathe became until it bordered on panic, and I'd gasp in the sweet relief of oxygen.

But I didn't feel any of that. I was almost calm. Staring at Dr. Harry. Listening to the quiet of the room. An old-fashioned clock ticked on the wall. I didn't breathe.

"Breathe. You're undoing everything we've done."

I took a scoop of air. "I don't know what we've done. You need to tell me." I pushed even more air out of my lungs and then didn't inhale.

He grabbed me by the shoulders and began to shake me saying, "Breathe. Breathe, damn you." I realized this was the first time I'd ever seen him emotional other than in my visions.

"Breathe!" he demanded one more time. And then let me go. His shoulders slumped. He stared at me, angry and raw. He didn't want to tell me what was happening to me. But he was also beginning to understand I wasn't going to cooperate unless I knew. We were playing a kind of medical chicken. Nervously, I wondered if I really wanted to win.

Then he began to speak. "You need to breathe because your cells won't function if you don't. And if they don't function, they could begin to decompose, *will* decompose. That's what we've been doing since the night you got here. Fighting decomposition."

"I'm decomposing? So I'm dead?"

He hesitated, then began slowly, "In a traditional sense, perhaps. Death is the cessation of vital function. Heartbeat, breathing, brain activity. As you know we're having trouble keeping your heart beating and your breathing is somewhat—optional. Your only reliable indication of life is brain activity. Consciousness."

"How did you do this?"

"I'll try to describe it as simply as I can. I believe I talked to you about microtubules when you first got here. Microtubules are the part of a cell that anesthesia acts upon to cause unconsciousness. They're also acted upon by so-called mind-expanding drugs like LSD." He paused, seeming to decide where to go next. "I began by researching AIDS. I lost someone close to me while I was in medical school. Many. I lost many people close to me. Friends, lovers. It was horrible."

"One of them was named Godwin?"

"Yes. My lover, William."

I didn't know what to say to that. Just knowing his lover's name seemed weirdly intimate. He continued, "There are many connections between HIV and cancer. The drugs used to treat both interfere with cellular processes. I suppose it's not surprising I eventually became interested in cancer research. Cancer drugs disrupt cellular function by attacking different parts of a cell. Some of them attack microtubules. I became attracted to that class of drugs, and eventually what I discovered evolved into Property Five."

"You destroyed part of my cells?"

"Quite the opposite. One of the drugs I was working with when I was researching cancer failed, but it failed in an interesting way. It fixed microtubules so that they're permanent. That part of each cell in your body appears to be indestructible. The rest of the cell, however, is subject to decomposition unless we find a way to keep your organ systems functioning."

I tried to take it all in. It was hard to grasp. "So you're trying to cure AIDS? Or cancer?"

"I'm trying to cure death."

My mouth fell open. Was he serious? I mean, it wasn't possible. You couldn't do something like that. No one lived forever. No one *should* live forever. I reached for something obvious and familiar. "You've turned me into a zombie."

He scowled. "Don't be ridiculous. Zombies are mythical. The religious fantasy of a primitive people."

They also ate human brains, and I barely ate. So I couldn't be a zombie. But what was I? Vampires were sort of dead and not dead. And they drank blood. Dr. Harry was having my blood treated and pumped back into me every day. Well, I thought it was my blood. Maybe it wasn't. Was I living on other people's blood? Was that what I was? A vampire? Of course, I was awake during the day and slept at night and could see myself in a mirror. Probably not a vampire.

This was bad, though. Really bad. I was thinking about horror movies trying to find some kind of role model. Holy shit.

"Are you all right?" Dr. Harry asked.

"Why would I be all right? You just told me I'm sort of not alive."

He ignored that. "Listen Jake, the work you and I have been doing in the last two weeks has been vitally important. Learning how to keep organ systems functional to prevent decomposition is crucial to our continuing this research. I can't in good conscience administer Property Five to anyone else until you've stabilized. Can I count on your cooperation?"

I nodded. I mean it wasn't like I had a choice. Cooperate or rot. That was a no-brainer.

"And I have your discretion?"

"I can't tell anyone?"

"No, you can't."

That was a little more challenging. How could I not tell Goth? He had a right to know. He was here, waiting around for the treatment. Maybe he didn't want to end up half dead just to be half alive. He should be told now so he could look around and see if any other options might help him stay alive. Actually, truly alive.

Of course, if he knew, if word got out everyone would know about me and I'd be this kind of freak. Forever.

twenty-nine

Okay, I'll be super honest. I should have figured it all out a lot sooner. But hey, *my life has turned into a twisted version of Frankenstein and I'm the monster* wasn't the first thing that popped into my head when things started going south. I mean, that's your basic paranoid schizophrenic territory, so usually it's a good idea to resist all thoughts of that nature.

In fact, I'm not so sure it's ever a good idea to be thinking those thoughts. I mean, maybe I was dead, or semi-dead, or whatever, or maybe I was just freaking crazy. Crazy being the preferable scenario.

When I got back to the ward, Goth lay in bed reading his Faulkner. The empty plates from his dinner sat on a tray next to his bed. The tray next to mine held a plate with a congealed mass of mashed potatoes and gravy. It made me glad I wasn't hungry. Except then I wondered if I'd ever be hungry again.

Goth looked up and saw me. "Hey, are you okay?"

"False alarm," I lied.

"Really? It seemed kind of serious." There was worry on his face, which I couldn't help thinking was sweet. I mean, it wasn't like we meant anything to each other. We were just two guys who tried to get it on and then didn't because one of their hearts stopped beating.

I pulled up the hem of my pajamas and showed him my ankles. They were a lovely shade of tomato instead of eggplant. I was working my way through the vegetable garden.

"So what happened?"

"It was a side effect. Completely normal." I climbed into my bed.

"Your heart didn't stop?"

"No. That would have been a whole lot more dramatic." To change the subject, I asked, "What happened to our heterosexual friend?"

"I took pity on him and walked him over to the girl's ward."

"Who's going to take pity on them?"

"Oh, I think they're fine. Three dying girls around our age, and no one's flirted with them in ions. I think they're actually appreciating Edmond's pathetic moves. If you get very quiet, you can hear them giggling."

We were quiet. He was right. Once or twice, I thought I heard giggling and snippets of Edmond's moves. Not that I thought, "Yo, you is hot" would get him anywhere.

"So you want to try again?" he asked. "We could go for a walk later."

"I think I need some down time. Maybe tomorrow."

"Okay," he said, trying not to sound disappointed but not doing such a good job. "Look, I'm sorry about the whole sex thing. I mean, I'm sort of a virgin. I didn't want to say that because, you know, 'I want lose my virginity before I die,' sounds like a dark, twisted high school comedy. I don't like the sum total of my life turning into something that trite, but when it comes down to it, that's sort of what my life is."

He was earnest and upset and worried he might have hurt me. His attempts at a wry smile made my heart do scary things again. But I liked him a lot, and at the same time I couldn't deal. I mean, up until a few weeks ago losing my virginity was an idea I'd completely given up on. When I began thinking I might live, it certainly moved up in importance but now, compared to maybe, sort of being some kind of undead freak, it seemed trivial again.

"Don't worry about it. No biggie," I said before I scooted down under my sheets. "I think I should maybe try to get some sleep."

"Sure thing." He went back to reading his book.

Closing my eyes, I pretended to sleep. I knew I couldn't, though. I had a lot to think about. This was so huge, I had trouble actually understanding it. I was dead, except I wasn't. I was alive but wasn't that, either. I was conscious. And the part of me that was conscious was going to continue. My life—as defined by my awareness of one moment after another—was going to continue, possibly, probably, for a very long time.

What would I do with all that time? Maybe my mom was right. Maybe I should become a doctor. If I did become a doctor, I promised myself I'd never use the word "optimistic." I'd tell my patients the absolute truth. No matter what. If they were going to die, I'd tell them that as kindly as I could.

Of course by the time I finished medical school, Property Five would be FDA approved and on the market. So all I'd ever have to say would be, 'You have a terrible illness. But don't worry, we'll give you Property Five. And you'll be fine. Dead, but fine.'

I heard Edmond huffing and puffing his way back into the ward. I kept my eyes closed. Goth got out of bed and helped him. Breathlessly, Edmond talked about the girls. "They're so hot, man. You should have stayed. I mean, there's one for each of us. I have, uh, dibs. Lea is the sexy one, and I am so in there. She wants me in the worst way. I could tell. I could just tell."

After Goth got Edmond into bed, Nurse Margie came in with Goth's nightly treatment: a plastic mouthpiece with an attachment he had to blow into. It looked kind of like a clear plastic kazoo. I cracked an eyelid to watch how he was doing. He seemed to be struggling. In between attempts, he would cough, a raspy, angry sound. Then he'd spit into a tissue.

Nurse Margie looked over at my bed. The look on her face would have made my blood run cold if it wasn't already running cold. Fear. She was afraid of me. I shut my eyes so she wouldn't see I was awake. That was weird. How much of the research did she understand? Given the way Dr. Harry treated her, I didn't think she knew much. She knew Dr. Harry had shocked me at a time when he shouldn't have, and I'd survived. Gotten better even. Had she guessed what I was? Would she guess? Could she?

Goth continued his struggle to clear his lungs. It sounded horrible and not terribly successful.

Nurse Margie said, "This isn't working as well as I'd like."

Then I heard her slapping something. I peeked again. She was slapping Goth on the back, practically beating him. She stopped and did it a few times on his chest. He didn't seem especially bothered by it. In fact, he looked bored. He caught me sneaking a look and shrugged his shoulders like he was saying, "Yeah, this happens."

He began coughing uncontrollably. This was what Property Five would save Goth from. Struggling to force up a lung full of mucus. Every day.

I felt a kind of excitement in my belly. Dr. Harry was going to give him Property Five. He was going to save Goth.

I was going to save Goth.

thirty

After Nurse Margie left, I stopped pretending to sleep and sat up to play games on my iPad. The best games required wi-fi so basically my choices sucked. I wanted something that would take up all my attention so I didn't have to think about what was going on with me.

When I was sixteen, I got addicted to WoW until my mother cancelled my subscription. I had an undead warrior I'd leveled up almost all the way to a hundred. It was a really good way not to think too much about having a terminal disease. Of course, playing an undead anything might not be such a great idea anymore. And since there was no wi-fi, I didn't exactly have to decide. My only real choice was solitaire. I poked around with the single-player, offline, boring game and eventually drifted off. Or at least it seemed like I'd drifted off.

"What you're doing here isn't right." It sounded like Nurse Margie. *Who was she talking to?*

Red seven on black eight. Move the two of diamonds to the ace of diamonds then the three.

"This is a research facility. Our methods may be difficult to understand." That was definitely Dr. Harry. He sounded tired, frayed, like he didn't want to be having this conversation.

"There's something very wrong with that boy. His vital signs are disturbing."

Draw a card. Ten of hearts. Useless. Draw again.

"I don't think you're qualified to judge."

"I've been a nurse for more than a decade. I think I can tell when a patient's vital signs—"

"And how many times have you been fired from your position?"

Jack of spades on the queen of diamonds.

"Dr. Harry, you said that didn't matter."

"It doesn't matter as long as you don't challenge my methods."

Flip through the pack. There has to be another move. Look for another move. Where was it? It had to be there.

"But the boy's vital—"

"Nurse."

"Yes, of course."

And then I must have fallen fully asleep because the next thing I knew it was very dark.

The sun had set hours before, and I was outside by the pond in the stony silence. Or was I? Was I really there? Darkness had swallowed the woods at the edge of the property, the double-wide, and most of the sky. It was calm. A cool wind blew in from the lake. Insects screeched. Frogs groaned. The vegetable garden lay still in the night. I stood at the foot of the raised garden and yet was not there. I was dreaming and not dreaming.

A tiny movement, a mound of dirt seemed to rise, clumps of rich soil rolling away. It reminded me of an anthill, a small pile of dirt surrounding a tiny tunnel. Except it wasn't an ant crawling out of the hole, it was a finger.

One pale, chalky finger struggling to pull itself farther out of the ground. And then there were two fingers. Old, gnarled fingers with cracked nails and thick knuckles and skin dried tight to the bone. The fingers flicked the dirt away and flicked and flicked until they became a hand, spreading all five fingers across the ground. Then the hand clawed and clawed until the wrist appeared.

A few feet away in another garden—that was clearly not a garden at all but a grave—another hand struggled to free itself. This one just as old, just as knotted. I watched, frozen, as the liver-spotted forearms dug their way out. An elbow. Two. Biceps. Shoulders. Lumps of dirt falling away, and the two ancient men who'd been my temporary roommates were pulling themselves out of the ground. Standing.

They reminded me of time-lapse photography showing how an onion grew, except they weren't vegetables. In fact, they were more animated now, more alive, than I'd ever seen them, as though being buried had given them strength, had nurtured them, had given them back life.

Shuffling away from the grave, dressed in thin hospital gowns streaked with damp soil, they walked toward the back of the Institute. Their bodies had swollen. Faces tight, empty of emotion, blurry almost. Moving. As though heading toward a beacon. A personal Mecca.

Something squirming around their eyes. Their ears. Something small and fleshy. Like tiny baby fingers. Yellow. Wiggling.

And then I realize the flies had gotten to them.

thirty-one

I woke. Breathing fast. Fear running through my body like it was a racetrack. I was safe in my bed, though. In the bed next to mine, Goth was absorbed in his book, while Edmond snored across from us. It was early, probably about an hour before breakfast. I looked over to see more than a dozen flies on the window screen. Waiting patiently. Waiting for me.

"You were having a bad dream," Goth said when he saw I was awake.

"I was."

I didn't think it was a big surprise I was having nightmares, specifically that sort of nightmare. Not after what Dr. Harry had told me. Why wouldn't I be dreaming about zombies? Maggot-filled zombies. Horrible zombies. Isn't that what I was afraid of becoming? *Could* I become that? I decided to stop that train of thought in its tracks. "How's your book?" I asked Goth.

"Heavy. I should have brought some supermarket books." My blank look made him add, "Trash."

"Don't you have an e-reader?"

"It's kind of crappy. And I've read everything on it. Can't download anything else in here. Since they've jammed reception."

"Jammed? No they—" I felt a little stupid for a moment. It wasn't just that they didn't have wi-fi and the reception was bad. They'd actually jammed it. "How did you figure that out?"

"Um, logic. They don't have wi-fi, that's easy to figure out. But there's also no cell service."

"We're in the boonies, though. Why would they have service?"

"Pretty much everywhere has service now. Plus, I've been wandering around on my cigarette breaks. At the very edge of the property, you can get a weak signal. If you follow it, it makes a circle around the Institute. They've got a jammer."

He adjusted his position so he could lean toward me, then whispered, "It's very illegal."

I almost asked why they'd do something like that. But I knew already. Dr. Harry didn't want word of his research getting out. Didn't want people figuring out what he was really doing and then texting about it. Putting up posts on Facebook. Twittering. @DrHarry Hey, dude. Heard you made the dead live. Totes cool.

Just then, Ray walked into the room pushing the vitals stand in front of him. He glanced at Edmond sleeping and then came over to Goth. As he put the blood pressure cuff around Goth's arm, I asked, "Where's Nurse Margie?"

"Gone."

"She was fired?"

He shrugged. "Or quit. Dunno."

"Are you a nurse?" Goth asked. It seemed a pertinent question.

"I'm just filling in for today. We called the agency. There will be a new nurse here tomorrow."

"I liked Nurse Margie," Goth said. "She was nice."

Ray started Goth's vitals. My mind struggled to grasp what this meant. Had my dream about Nurse Margie talking with Dr. Harry been real? Had I heard part of a conversation that had ended in Nurse Margie being fired?

"What did she do?" I asked. "To get fired?"

"I told you, I don't know if she got fired. She might have quit. She's got that kid who takes up a lot of her time."

"But then she would have given notice, wouldn't she?"

"Maybe. I dunno." Ray stuck a thermometer into Goth's mouth and tried to look like he knew what he was doing as he took Goth's pulse.

"So what *might* she have done?" I asked.

Ray gave me an uncomfortable look. I expected him to say I was asking too many questions because I was. But then he said, "Dr. Harry asked me to fill in because Nurse Margie isn't here anymore. Then he reminded me about the thing I signed about keeping my mouth shut. So, you know, even if I did know why she got fired, I wouldn't tell you. Now would I?"

"Dr. Harry was afraid she was going to say something she shouldn't," I said, half to myself. Except that might not be right because firing her would pretty much guarantee she'd run her mouth at every opportunity. So was it safe to fire her? It certainly wasn't safe to keep her around. "Have you talked to Nurse Margie since it happened?"

"Sure, we're best buds. We don't do much but talk on the phone all day." When he was done being snotty, he made notations on Goth's chart then moved around the bed and came over to me.

I wondered if Dr. Harry had had to give Nurse Margie a lot of money. Wasn't that the way it worked? If you wanted someone to keep quiet, you gave them a bunch of money and threatened to take it away if they said anything. Of course, we'd already signed a—

"But everybody has to sign a non-disclosure agreement, right? Even the staff?" Goth asked, his thoughts tracking my own. Great minds, you know?

"Yeah," said Ray. "So we need to stop talking about that kind of shit. We'll all get in trouble."

I was going to ask a question about how binding those agreements really were when Ray jammed the thermometer into my mouth.

"So what exactly goes on upstairs?" Goth asked.

"Testing," Ray said.

"What do the tests say?"

Ray gave him a puzzled look. "They say the kind of things test say. You know whether someone's normal."

"And are we? Are we normal?"

"Of course not. If you were normal, who'd want to study you?" He had a point. He also hadn't told us anything we didn't already know.

He took the thermometer out of my mouth. Frowned at it. Stuck it back in.

I pushed it to one side with my tongue and said, "I'd like to see Dr. Harry later. Can you make that happen?"

Maybe I'd tell him about my dreams or maybe I'd just ask questions about Nurse Margie's sudden departure. Or both.

"I'm sorry, he's not available today," Ray said, and I suddenly had a vision of Ray as a nurse. He'd be the kind who enjoyed saying no and reveled in anything that 'might pinch a little.'

"Tomorrow, then."

"There will be a new nurse in the morning. Talk to her about it." Removing the thermometer again, he studied it then wrote down the result. "Your temperature's lower than it was yesterday." He considered for a moment, then added, "That doesn't make sense."

I couldn't resist messing with him a bit. "You just said I wasn't normal. Why would my temperature be normal?"

He just looked at me for a moment before he put the blood pressure cuff on my arm. He pressed the button on the vitals stand, and it began to pump up.

"That's not going to be normal either."

"Quiet."

I was quiet.

Looking over at Goth, I rolled my eyes. He smirked. Why was everything feeling so ordinary? After the things Dr. Harry said the day before, shouldn't I be freaking out? I mean, being told you don't fulfill all the requirements for life should cause a little anxiety, right? But I wasn't that anxious. I *felt* alive. And I guess if you *feel* alive, it's hard to think of yourself as not alive.

Ray released the blood pressure cuff. From the look on his face, I figured it was just as scary low as my temperature. He studied the chart for a moment, and then he said, "Dr. Harry wants me to look at your ankles."

He pulled down the thin blanket and the sheet. His face kind of contorted. "Jesus Christ."

I looked down at my exposed feet. Oddly, my first thought was how much they looked like my mother's feet. Narrow with long toes. Though much, much bigger. The skin tone wasn't too bad, a little pale maybe. But the thing that got Ray swearing was that my feet were filthy, covered in dirt and bits of grass. It took a moment for me to understand what that meant, and in that moment fear crept over me.

I hadn't been dreaming of being out back at all. I'd really been out there. I'd really watched as those two old men, those two old, maggoty, dead men rose from their garden graves and headed toward the Institute. But what had happened? Had they made it to the building? Had something stopped them? Where were they now?

"Looks like someone's been sleepwalking," Goth said.

<h1 style="text-align:center">thirty-two</h1>

I went to the bathroom attached to the ward to wash my feet. Ray was gone when I got back. Edmond was sitting up in bed, Ray having obviously woken him to get his vitals. Slinking back to my bed, I felt super embarrassed. It was one thing to have these weird wanderings when it was just me who knew about them, but now Goth knew. Well, he didn't know, not really. He didn't know what I'd seen.

Climbing into bed, I realized Ray hadn't changed my sheets. I'd probably have to wait for Miss Haggerty to come in. She'd be annoyed and diffident no matter how nicely I asked her, but at least she'd do it. Using the remote, I lifted the bed so I could sit up and curl my legs underneath me so I didn't have to stick my nice, clean feet in the grime at the foot of my bed.

"You didn't see me, you know, getting out of bed?" I asked Goth.

"No. Kinda weird. I don't sleep all that well."

Actually, no one slept that well around him, either. He sort of hacked and coughed his way through the night.

"Have you always been a sleepwalker?"

"Sleepwalker?" Edmond asked. "Who's a sleepwalker?"

"Jake has been walking in his sleep," Goth explained.

"I haven't done it in a really long time," I said. It was a total lie. I'd never been a sleepwalker. It was just easier to let Goth and Edmond think I was one than clue them into what was really going on.

"You think the girls are awake yet?" Edmond asked, but he still had sleep in his voice. Goth shrugged, and Edmond rolled over and was snoring again two seconds later.

"You want to watch a movie?" Goth asked me.

"Sure. Where do you want to watch it? In the solarium?"

"No, it's too bright in there. Let's just do it here." He scooted over in his bed. There wasn't a lot of room but there was enough. I crossed the few feet to Goth's bed and climbed up in.

He handed me a stack of his DVDs and told me to go ahead and pick one. I looked through them: *Love Story*, *Brian's Song*, *Terms of Endearment*, *Dark Victory*, *Pride of the Yankees*. I didn't know all of the movies, but I quickly scanned the synopses. I only read a couple before I picked up the theme.

"You're kidding me."

"Art teaches us who to be."

"You don't need to learn how to die young. It sort of happens whether you want it to or not."

"But I *do* need to know how." He had a kind of smirk on his face, so I wasn't sure he was all that serious.

"I don't think I've seen any of these movies, but my guess is that the dying person dies nobly and with dignity."

"Exactly. I want to learn how to do that. Left to my own devices, I might just sit in the corner and cry."

"But you're here. Trying to live."

"I've got my fingers crossed. Hopefully the DVDs are more plan B than they used to be."

I decided to go with *Love Story*, assuming at least part of it would be romantic. Sitting together in Goth's bed, we got a couple of sidelong glances from Ray as he came in and out, but he didn't say anything. Edmond woke up long enough to get Goth to promise to walk him over to the girl's ward in the afternoon. Goth munched on Lorna Doones. When he offered me one, he gave the name a cheesy Irish accent.

Shaking my head, I asked him, "Where do you get them?"

"I just ask for them. You can ask for whatever you want. Nurse Margie will get it for you. Or whoever it is who replaces her. Hopefully." That made us somber for a moment. If we got another Ray or Miss Haggerty, it wasn't likely Goth would ever see a cookie again.

"What's your favorite cookie?" he asked.

"I dunno."

"You don't know what your favorite cookie is?"

"I used to like anything with mint. But right now it sounds terrible."

"Ask the new nurse for some tomorrow. Experiment. If you still don't want them, I'll eat them."

We went back to watching the movie. Ali McGraw was calling Ryan O'Neal preppy like it was his name. I fell asleep with my head on Goth's shoulder around the time she announced that, "Love means never having to say you're sorry."

Even in my virginal state, I knew that was a crock. In fact, being in love probably meant you had to say you're sorry a lot more than normal people. Apologizing might have gone a long way to fixing my parents' marriage.

I did actually sleep through Ali's getting sick and dying, which honestly wasn't such a disappointment.

I woke up in the middle of a relatively normal dream in which I was chased up a staircase that went nowhere. It was the kind of dream that used to scare the crap out of me but was now reassuringly mundane. And vague. And in no way, shape or form possible.

But then I realized something. The fact that my feet were dirty didn't mean the old men had been buried in the back. It just meant I went outside in my sleep. I could have been dreaming about the old men while I was sleepwalking. Right? And as soon as I thought that I felt a lot better. It made sense.

The old men weren't real.

They couldn't be real. They'd disappeared a while ago. If they had been buried in the backyard, why would it take so long for them to dig their way out? I guess they could have been buried really deep. Or maybe they weren't buried right away. I stopped myself. This was really stupid shit to think about. I dreamed the old men. They were in some nursing home somewhere. Just like Nurse Margie said they were.

"Do you want me to go back to the part where you fell asleep?" Goth asked, reaching for his closed DVD player.

"No, that's okay," I said. "What did she die of?"

"Old movie disease."

"What is that?"

"It's where they never say what you have, but you never look bad and the lighting's always great."

"Oh. That sounds nice." I should have gone back to my bed, but I was comfortable. Very comfortable. Then I asked him the question I'd been asking myself: "So if the treatment works on you, what do you want to do with your life?"

"I just want to get old. Preferably not alone. I want to live long enough for my hair to turn gray and fall out. I want to get fat and misshapen. I want to grunt when I stand up and fart too much and complain about the pain in my joints. I want my skin to get thin and papery and my eyes hazy. And I want to live the kind of life that earns you those things. A long one."

"Me too."

I wondered if I was lying. I didn't know much about what would happen to me. I didn't know for sure if I could get old. Once Dr. Harry got my organ systems balanced and functioning correctly, would I age? I had no idea. Did I want to be nineteen forever? Oh God, probably not. But was there anything I could do about it? There was so much I needed to ask. And so much I was afraid to ask.

A lot of things that normally happened didn't happen that day. Ray only did some of the things Nurse Margie would have done. Goth didn't get his back-slapping treatment. I did get my afternoon stem cell treatment, but no blood was taken in the morning. Edmond was basically ignored.

When the afternoon rolled around, I lay drowsily back in my own bed, taking in my treated blood. Goth decided to walk Edmond over to the girl's ward. They could have waited so I could have gone to meet the girls, too, but...I don't know, I wasn't especially into making new friends.

Having secrets will do that, I guess.

Left alone in the silence, I let my mind drift. I could hear Goth and Edmond as they walked, even after they left the ward. *I heard Edmond ask, "So, are you guys like fags or something?"*

"Yeah, we are," Goth replied.

"Oh. Okay. That's cool." It took him all of five seconds to realize, "Holy shit, that means I have the girls all to myself."

"It sure does."

"Awesome."

I had to chuckle. Edmond was kind of a jerk and kind of not a jerk. I guess he was just like the rest of us. Trying to be the person he thought he was supposed to be whether that was really who he wanted to be or not.

I guess I did that, too. My mom wanted me to get better, so I played the good patient figuring that was how to get better. But was that who I really was? Maybe it all would have been easier if I'd screamed and yelled every time I wanted to give up. Or maybe it would have been a lot harder. I wasn't sure.

"What you're saying is that you've halted the study until you're certain this one subject is going to, what was the word you used? Thrive?" The man speaking was on a computer screen. Skype? Facetime? Google-whatever. One of those apps.

"I don't know why you're having trouble understanding this. I spoke clearly enough." That was Dr. Harry. He sat at his desk staring at the computer. His arms crossed his chest. He was obviously annoyed with the man on the screen, who was younger than Dr. Harry and better groomed.

"I'm having trouble understanding why you think you can make that decision unilaterally. I thought we had a partnership."

"We do have a partnership, Dr. Callabray, but the study is my purview."

"That's not how this is supposed to work. Your purview is Property Five. You've done it. You've perfected the treatment, and it extends life, just as you'd hoped. Now it's our turn to develop the protocols that will guarantee quality of life. But we can't do that with just one test subject."

"You're going to have to."

Dr. Harry sat back in his chair and seemed to consider for a moment. Then, slowly, he said, "I cannot play Russian roulette with people's lives."

"But isn't that what you're doing? Keeping subjects out of your study could be equally disastrous. In this situation, the only way you can truly know the ethical choice would be to see the future. Can you see the future, Dr. Harry?"

"No. I can't."

"Then you should proceed with other subjects."

"No. I won't. I took an oath. First do no—"

"Oh, don't be ridiculous. If you took that seriously, you wouldn't have come this far."

"I don't know that I've done the right thing. I've taken risks. Risks I perhaps should not have taken. I won't risk making things worse for my subjects."

"You've chosen subjects who are going to die very soon. How much worse can it get?"

"It could get worse. It could get much worse."

"I'm going to have to discuss this with my investors."

"Yes. I was expecting that."

Goth came back into the ward, which woke me. I sat up in bed in time to see him looking at me funny, reading my face.

"What's wrong?"

"Nothing. I fell asleep again. I was dreaming."

Was I dreaming? It all felt so real. But then it felt real in the way a TV show feels real, which wasn't real at all.

Then Goth said, "Edmond put two and two together and figured out we're gay."

"Yeah, I know."

"What do you mean, you know?"

I wasn't sure what to say for a moment. I couldn't tell him I'd overheard a conversation that should have been impossible for me to overhear. Finally, I said, "I meant that it's logical he'd figure it out, that's all."

Then I realized, if I did actually overhear their conversation, maybe the dreams weren't dreams at all. And I wasn't dreaming about the conversation I'd dreamed Dr. Harry having. It was real. And it was me they were talking about. I was the subject who wasn't thriving. The study wasn't going well. I wasn't getting better. And if I wasn't getting better, that meant that I was decomposing. And if I was decomposing...

"It could get worse. It could get much worse." Dr. Harry had said.

I didn't want to believe him.

thirty-three

Okay, so maybe it's kind of weird I hadn't spent a lot more time trying to figure out why I was suddenly telepathic or dreamapathic or whatever. But let's be honest, I had a few things on my mind and absolutely no access to Google. Not that I had a clue about what search terms to use: WHAT HAPPENS WHEN YOU DIE BUT DON'T? LONGTERM NEAR DEATH EXPERIENCES? SUBVERTING DEATH? Even if I did have the Internet, it might not have been helpful.

Not much happened the rest of the week. The nurse from the agency arrived. Her name was Kelly. She was very young, only about a year or so older than me, I think. Her skin was pink and creamy, and she always looked like she'd just woken up. She wasn't as clueless as Ray, but I did get the feeling sometimes she wanted to run and check her class notes.

Goth and I watched a few more movies from his sack. He had a couple in there that weren't about death: *Notting Hill, Four Weddings and a Funeral*—well the second one did have a little death in it but it was sudden and over quickly. Then Goth wasn't doing so great and had to spend a whole day on oxygen.

Nurse Kelly kept coming in and readjusting it until he snapped at her that it was fine. We called her Nurse Kelly even though she wanted us to call her just plain Kelly. She corrected us a lot on Wednesday but by Friday had given up. She was Nurse Kelly whether she wanted to be or not.

Goth took Edmond over to see the girls another time. And then, when he got sicker, Nurse Kelly walked Edmond over. I could have taken him, but I didn't really want to. I still wasn't in any big rush to get to know the girls. It was too weird being the guinea pig everyone was waiting on. It was bad enough Goth and Edmond were watching me, hoping I was improving, because that meant they'd be improving soon.

I hadn't improved much, though, and it felt like I was letting everyone down. My heart hadn't stopped again. That was in the plus column. I was managing to breathe, at least when I remembered. My appetite sucked. Anything to do with food going into me and coming out of me was just, well, I don't even want to think about it. I was bloated, so I felt fat even though I was probably pretty skinny. Mostly I liked staying in bed and being still. Which wasn't good. Wasn't good at all.

And I was still hearing things I shouldn't. The girls talking about TV shows they missed and wished they could see. Dr. Harry should at least get cable. Once or twice, Miss Haggerty made a call in the middle of the night and told someone they were a "real fucker." I had no idea what that was about.

By Friday afternoon, I'd started wondering if I might be able to somehow control the dreams. I mean, why not? It was better than just lying in bed. Actually, I'd still be lying in bed but it was at least lying in bed with a purpose.

Sometime around year two of acute-blah-blah-blah-leukemia my mother started bringing home all these new age books she thought would help me think myself well again. To get her off my back, I spent a lot of time relaxing my entire body, imagining myself on an idyllic desert island and then slowly, carefully imagining a yellow bubble working its way through every single part of my body.

It didn't work. Obviously. And at first, my mom was convinced I hadn't really tried. Which was kind of silly since it wasn't exactly hard to imagine a yellow bubble. Still, she made me do it again and again until she finally gave up.

So, it wasn't all that difficult for me to relax my entire body and then just let what happened happen. The noises around me—Goth's movie leaking out of his earbuds, Nurse Kelly tapping a pen as she did a cross-word puzzle at the front desk, cars going by, flies dive-bombing the window screen—all faded away. It was a little harder to push away my fear of what would happen next, but I did it.

There was nothing but me, the conscious me, sliding off the bed and drifting out of the ward. I tried to focus hard on where I wanted to go. Upstairs. That's where I wanted to go. I wanted to go into all the rooms I'd never been in. I passed jaundiced-Jesus and floated up the steps to the second floor. There were a lot of doors. I tried the first one to my right. It was a closet filled with a mop and a bucket. I sort of giggled and eased my way back to the hallway. I tried the door on the other side. That put me into a laboratory.

I looked around. It was nearly as big as the ward I was in. There were two counters with some kind of indestructible-looking black stone on them. You would want it to be, I suppose. In case you accidentally made some sort of acid that ate through things or blew up a petri dish. Each counter had a sink at one end and a couple of gas nozzles so you could heat up chemicals. Or your lunch.

Other than that, the countertops were bare. It didn't look like anyone was doing much in the way of experimenting at the moment. Each counter had a lot of drawers. I wondered if Property Five was in any of them. I also wondered how exactly I would find out since I couldn't open the drawers any more than I could open the door.

The problem was solved when I turned around and noticed a small cabinet with a glass door standing behind me against the wall. Inside I could see a white box, open at the top, with around twenty small vials filled with clear fluid. That was it. It didn't need a label. I remembered Dr. Harry holding the vial to the light. That was what I was looking for. Looking the cabinet over, I noticed it was padlocked. Which was weird. Did Dr. Harry really think someone might break in and steal it here, in the middle of nowhere?

Suddenly, a key turned in the door. Someone was coming. I pushed myself up against the wall, afraid of being caught. And then remembered I was there and not there. I wouldn't be seen by whoever—

Miss Haggerty walked into the laboratory. It was early in the day for her to be there for her shift, though. She wore her street clothes, a dark blue Spartan's T-shirt over a pair of black yoga pants. She went right for a filing cabinet on the far side of the laboratory.

Taking out a key, she unlocked the glass cabinet. On the shelves above Property Five were rows of medications in plastic bottles. Miss Haggerty took two bottles of medication from the second shelf from the top, slipped them into a pocket, then carefully lined the bottles up so they were all at the front and no one would notice any were missing. Over her shoulder, I read the bottle. Morphine. Extended release.

Apparently, Miss Haggerty had a little problem with drugs.

She locked the cabinet, returned the key to the file drawer and scurried out of the room. Then I wondered about something. Did Dr. Harry know? There was something weird about the people who worked at the Institute. Nurse Margie had had a spotty work history and a big mouth. Ray didn't seem to know what he was doing. Nurse Kelly was barely older than I was. And now, Miss Haggerty—

Dr. Harry was scraping the bottom of the barrel. Was he doing it deliberately? Knowing they were desperate, knowing their problems, did he think they were easy to manipulate? Did he know they would do his bidding?

thirty-four

Saturday morning, we slogged through our basic routine. Breakfast, vitals, pills, blood, it was getting kind of repetitive. I fell asleep while Nurse Kelly was taking my blood and didn't wake up until well after she was done. Goth wasn't in his bed and neither was Edmond. I was pretty certain I knew where they both were: Edmond was making time with the girls, and Goth was outside smoking.

I climbed out of bed and dragged myself through the Institute until I got to the back. Just outside the back door, I found Goth leaning against the back of the building, a cigarette hanging from his mouth.

"Are you feeling better?"

He shrugged. "Not exactly. But I lied to Nurse Kelly, and she let me come out here."

"Can I have one of those?" I asked. Maybe it would keep the flies off me.

"No. You're not really a smoker. And this isn't exactly what you'd call a good time to start."

"Is there a good time to start smoking?" I said, swatting at a fly.

"Cute. Look you're just getting—"

"Don't be an asshole, just give me a cigarette."

With another shrug, he offered me the pack and his lighter. I lit it and managed to inhale without coughing but God it was disgusting. *Why did people do this?* It tasted like I'd licked asphalt. I wanted to just throw it away, but I did think it would keep the flies from bothering me. Not many people could use that as an excuse for smoking.

"I told Nurse Kelly I wanted to get some exercise. Can we walk a little so I'm not a liar?"

"Sure. I don't mind."

"Just not fast."

We walked out past the double-wide on our way to the pond. I asked him, "You're having trouble breathing?"

"Always. It's okay, though. I'm due for percussion therapy. That might help."

"Percussion therapy? That's what they call it? Sounds like you're a drum."

"It feels like I'm a drum."

"You want me to do it?"

"No. Nurse Kelly will do it later."

The pond was to our right. I could tell he wanted to stop there for a minute but I figured the cigarette smoke would only keep the flies off me for so long, so I kept walking.

"How do *you* feel? Are you doing okay?" Goth asked. There was hopefulness in his voice that worried me. I needed to get better to save him.

"I'm okay. Better."

I wasn't better, though. At best I was the same.

We reached the raised gardens. I stood at the foot of them, staring down. The two tilled gardens looked different than they had the last time we were there. Different than they had in my dream. In two of the gardens, the ground had settled and sunk. As though something had been removed. And maybe something had been.

A breeze meandered in from Lake Michigan. Cool and moist. The very back of the property was mainly a small, lazy hill covered in clumps of grass. I scanned it, looking for I don't know what. Then I noticed something—

"Why are we looking at the garden?" Goth asked.

"I wanted to see if anything was growing."

"It's the beginning of September. Things are going to stop growing soon."

Ignoring him, I trudged up the little hill. There, just at the top, was a spot where the ground had been turned. It was about two-foot by two-foot. Obviously, it wasn't a garden. Someone had dug a hole and buried something. I looked up and noticed another turned spot about fifteen feet away. I went over to it. Goth fell behind, unable to keep up. I stared at this new spot then looked up to scan the grounds for another spot. I found one. Then another.

I lurched from hole to hole, spotting more each time I stopped. At least twelve small holes, maybe more, had recently been dug and something buried in them. A horrible feeling crept up my spine, across the back of my neck and grabbed me by the throat.

The old men *had* dug themselves out of their graves. They'd tried to get into the institute. But someone had stopped them. And that someone had buried them again. In a dozen different places. In pieces.

Goth was fifty feet away. I was near the double-wide, hurried over, climbed onto the deck and opened the sliding glass door. I rushed through the kitchen, the living room, and then I was standing in front of the walk-in door. The refrigerated room. I hadn't thought about it at all since I'd first seen it. I mean, a lot had happened. But now, now it seemed like the most important thing in the world. I looked down at the handle ready to pull open the door. But someone had put a padlock on it. When had that happened? Why had it happened? What was in there?

I hurried back to the kitchen, began opening drawers and cabinets, but they were mostly empty. A dish, a bowl, nothing that would—and then I found what I needed under the sink. A small, red fire extinguisher.

I grabbed it and hurried back to the refrigerated room. I smashed the extinguisher into the lock. It took a few tries, but the lock finally broke. I pulled it off, threw it aside, dropped the extinguisher, and opened the door.

Inside it was cold, very cold. So cold even I noticed. On one side of the walk-in stood a set of shelves with mostly plastic tubs sitting on them. On the other side a gurney. Whatever was on it was covered in a sheet. It was probably a body, a corpse.

I decided to look into the tubs first. I pulled one out. In it was a frog pinned to a board just the way we'd done in ninth grade science. It was partially dissected. Its chest was open; it's internal organs exposed. They were dried out, desiccated. I wondered why someone would save something like that. Then its head moved. It looked at me. I jumped back pushing the tub away from me.

There were half a dozen other tubs. I couldn't look into them. Imagining what might be in them was enough. Knowing seemed worse. At the far end was some kind of cage with a checked tablecloth partially draped over it. Something inside the cage moved. I couldn't stop myself puling the tablecloth off.

Inside were a dozen white mice. They turned their heads toward me when the cloth came off. Each in various stages of decomposition. Fur patchy. Skin taut. An odor wafted from the cage. It was the smell of rot, food turning, carcasses fermenting in the sun. It reminded me of garbage bins and unwashed alleys. I stepped back. Not wanting to be close to the mice.

Then something touched me.

thirty-five

I was outside standing on the deck when Goth got to the double wide.

"What's going on?" he asked. "You look weird."

"Nothing's going on," I said. Even though a lot was going on.

I was fairly certain the little girl I'd seen was inside the double-wide, lying on a gurney and that she'd touched me. I probably could have pulled back the sheet to be sure, but I hadn't wanted to know. Knowing meant I should do something, but there was nothing I could do.

"Let's go in there," he suggested pointed at the double wide.

I didn't want to go back in. I'd broken the lock on the walk-in refrigerator. I was afraid the things inside would try to get out. "Let's just hang out here." I sat down on the edge of the deck. He came over and sat beside me.

"There's more privacy inside."

I couldn't think of a good reason not to go inside the double-wide, so I threw myself on Goth and started kissing him. His lips were fever hot, like they'd been before. Only now I knew why. There wasn't anything wrong with him. It was me. All me. I was cold, anything warm felt hotter than it was. What did Goth feel? I knew I was cold to the touch. Did he think everyone was as cold as I was? Did he think this was what kissing was like with everyone? We kissed for nearly a whole minute and then I pushed him off me.

"Can't breathe."

"Oh, sorry."

Actually, I didn't need to breathe which I guess might come in handy when making out. Just then, though, I needed a moment to collect my thoughts. Or at least change gears. The things I'd just seen. The thing that had touched—

"How's your heart?" Goth asked.

"Beating."

"Good," he puffed. "Maybe you're right. Maybe this isn't the right time for privacy. You're probably doing better than I am right now."

"Let's just hang out then."

He took my arm and tucked it around him so that my hand was in the center of his chest. But then he started coughing. Eventually he spit into a tissue, wadding it up and putting it back into his bathrobe pocket.

"Sorry. That's disgusting, I know."

"No biggie," I said. It was hardly as disgusting as the things I'd just seen. In fact, it was completely normal. I mean, everyone hacked things up now and then. It was just life. What I'd seen wasn't life. It was half-life. Shit, I thought, what I'd seen were things like me. The frogs, the mice, the girl, me. We were the same. Half alive, half dead.

Pulling me closer Goth said, "Can I tell you something? I think Dr. Harry brought you here for me. Because we're both gay."

"So, this is like the creepiest blind date ever?"

He shrugged. "I guess. It's my first blind date."

"Do you mind?" I asked.

"I don't mind. I like you. Do you like me?"

"I do like you. It's just that I have a lot going on."

"That's what's kind of cool about this. Us," he said. "We both have a lot going on. I'm not sure I'd want to be with a regular boy. He wouldn't understand, and he might feel sorry for me. You don't. You get it."

I squeezed him tighter, and he squeezed me back. We fell silent and I began thinking about everything I'd seen. The old men buried in pieces. Dr. Harry's failed experiments. And that's when it hit me. It really hit me. *I* couldn't die. But the way things were going, I couldn't exactly live.

I had a horrifying thought. My body was decomposing while my mind, my consciousness remained strong and aware. What had Dr. Harry done to me? Even if he stabilized me, someday I'd grow old, my body would wear out, then what would happen? Would I end up buried in some fetid coffin completely aware for all eternity? Oh my God, that sounded so, so shitty.

That's why Dr. Harry didn't want to give anyone else the treatment. He didn't know how to stabilize a person after their microtubules had been fixed. He didn't know how to stop the decomposition. Some of it worked, some of it worked a little, and some of it didn't work at all. If Dr. Harry didn't fix this, I was simply going to disintegrate.

thirty-six

"I can't die, can I?" I asked Dr. Harry when he called me into the examining room later that morning. He looked tired, worn. The good looks I'd seen floating below the surface seemed to have fled. I wasn't sure, but I think he smelled like booze. My question stopped his exam. He took a step back and considered his answer.

"That's a matter of definition. As long as—"

"Stop with the medical doublespeak. I can't die, can I?"

"I'm not sure. It's not the kind of thing I can set up an experiment for." Well, those were terrible words to hear from a doctor.

"How about an educated guess?"

"It could be very difficult for you to die. Yes."

"But you can't stop the decomposition, can you?"

He stepped back to me and began to check the lymph nodes in my neck. "As I said before, the work you and I are doing is—"

"I'm not doing any *work*. I'm being experimented on. That's a lot different than work." My voice was louder than I wanted it to be. I was angry. Angry in a way I hadn't been for a long time.

He sighed and tried to continue. I pushed his hands away.

"Please calm down, Jake. You knew this was a research facility when you came here."

"This isn't what I signed up for."

"But it is. It's exactly what you signed up for. The risks were outlined in the agreement you signed and sent in before you even came here."

"That was with the non-disclosure agreement?"

"It outlined—"

"Yeah. My mom forged my signature. I never saw any of it."

"Oh. I see. The agreement outlined the risks involved up to and including death. Your mother said—"

"Don't worry about what my mom said. Did the agreement mention that I could get caught between life and death?"

"Not explicitly."

"Then it doesn't matter what my mom did or didn't tell me, does it? We know she didn't tell me that." I was quiet, then said, "We're in uncharted territory, aren't we?"

The beginning of *Star Trek* popped into my head. I heard Kirk going on about boldly going where no man has gone before. All those times I watched the show, it never occurred to me that being the first to go anywhere might be a really, really stupid idea.

"You're right, Jake. I don't know what will happen next." Quietly he went on, "I wanted, I hoped...can you imagine a world without loss? A world without grief? It would be a wonderful place, don't you think?"

Something fell into place. "The pictures in your office. That's what this is all about. You lost—"

"What? Wait— How do you know that? You've never been in my office."

"Oh, I, um, snuck in once after my PET scan."

"No. You didn't. I keep the office locked."

I don't know why I thought it but I felt like telling him the truth was going to make things so much worse than they were. I scrambled to think of something to say but came up empty.

"How did you know about the pictures?" His voice was flat, hollow.

I didn't have another lie, so I told the truth. "I have these kinds of dreams."

"Dreams? You dreamed about the pictures in my office?"

"Maybe vision is a better word. I had a vision. I thought maybe I was imagining them. But they're there, aren't they?"

He nodded.

Actually, it was a relief to tell him about the dreams. I had the fleeting thought he might be able to stop them. "Sometimes it's like I'm sleepwalking, and sometimes it's like I'm traveling outside my body."

"Astral projection."

"Is that what it's called?"

"It's pseudoscience." Tentatively, he went back to examining me. Checking my pulse. Reassuring himself by collecting true scientific data. "Apparently, people in deep meditative states feel their consciousness leaves their body. There's no scientific support for these types of experiences."

"But isn't that what you've done to me? My consciousness is alive while my body is dying. You've separated them."

"Perhaps. They've done studies in rats that indicate brain activity increases near death."

I flashed on the white mice he had hidden in a cage. Did they have weird dreams, too? Poor dreaming, rotting mice.

"So, I'm telepathic because I'm dying?"

"Not dying exactly. More like in a persistent state of dying."

That was too big to think about. A persistent state of dying. I can't tell you how bad that sounded.

"The therapeutic cloning of your cells has shown some success. Our partners have been grafting your fixed microtubules to living cells that have the capability to regenerate. It works in some—"

"You're talking about Dr. Callabray?"

He stopped and stared at me, afraid. I'd frightened him. I'd frightened my doctor. That was weird. I'd seen pity, compassion, and distaste but never fear. I didn't like the way that felt. His looking at me with fear in his eyes, his looking at me like I might explode, would explode, at any moment.

Then he continued, "So far it depends on what type of cell we're talking about. Corneal cells, for instance. We've been very successful with those. When a body decomposes, the eyes quickly become opaque as the corneal cells decompose. That's never happened to you."

I'd had about as much as I could deal with, so I got down off the table. Even though I was starting to have an earache I wasn't in the mood to be poked and prodded. As I pushed by him, Dr. Harry asked, "Where are you going?"

"You need to go out to the double wide. The lock on the refrigerated unit got broken. You don't want anyone to get out."

"You were in there? You saw...?"

"Yes. I saw the girl. Who is she?"

"She's the child of one of the neighbors. I heard she'd died and then two days later— Things went well for a while, they really did, I was hopeful. But you see what happened."

"Where do her parents think her body is?"

"They don't know anything about the work we do here. No one does. Ray and I took the girl from the funeral home in the middle of the night. It's his family's business. It's quite the scandal locally."

"I'm sure that's comforting to her parents."

"It's not. I know that. I tried to do something kind, and it turned out badly."

"She opens her eyes. She moves."

"Yes, that's all she does."

thirty-seven

Late Saturday afternoon, my parents arrived. Together.

Which was kind of odd. Okay, understatement. It was super odd, stupendously odd, epically odd. I could not for the life of me remember the last time I'd seen them in the same room. Seriously, my parents only spoke to each other on the phone. Yeah, they spoke often. But always about me—my health, mainly, occasionally about my happiness but usually only my health—and that was it. They never asked about each other. They didn't have coffee to catch up. They didn't get together on my birthday. They kept their distance. Seeing them in the same place at the same time wasn't normal. And I could tell from their body language, they agreed.

Even though he now works for law firms, my dad looks pretty much like what he really is: a musician. His hair is too long, and he has a tattoo of a Gibson Flying V electric guitar on his forearm. It's just like the one Jimi Hendrix used. My dad was born after Hendrix died, so the fact that he even knows who Hendrix was is weird. And the fact that I know is even weirder. Well, my dad talked about him enough, so maybe it's not that weird—okay, I looked him up on Wikipedia like three times.

My mom came over to the bed and kissed me on the cheek and then my dad came over and said, "Hey buddy," trying to do a funky handshake he'd taught me when I was a kid. But after he gripped my hand, he stopped.

"Holy shit. You're ice cold." He turned to my mom and said, "He's ice cold."

"Bobby, it's fine. The doctor knows all about it."

"You knew about this?"

I rushed in with, "It's not a big deal. It's a side effect of the treatment." I didn't need my dad getting all worried about me. Didn't need him pulling me out of the Institute and taking me to a real hospital where I'd just—

"Jake, introduce your father," my mom said, nodding her head toward Goth.

"That's G—"

"What's your temperature?" my father demanded. He wasn't going to give up. Poor Goth couldn't take his eyes off us. Probably because we were this total train wreck. I wanted to pull the covers over my head.

"My temperature is just a few degrees below normal."

"A few? How many?"

I shrugged. "I don't know. Four maybe." It was more like seven.

"That's hypothermia."

"Oh, good God, how do you even know that?" My mom was annoyed, though to be fair she was probably annoyed the minute they got into the same car. I couldn't imagine them driving up from Chicago together. What a nightmare.

"I know that because I read a book on mountain climbers. Half of them died of hypothermia."

"Well, Jake is not dying. Look at him."

My dad gave me a good look. "He looks pale."

"Pale is not dying. He hasn't been outside in ages. Of course he's pale."

Not exactly true. I had been outside a couple of times, but I wasn't going to tell her that.

"And—" my dad started.

"And what?"

"Well, he looks a little...greenish."

"Oh, he does not. The lighting in here is terrible. That's all."

"What kind of doctor is this Dr. Hairy?"

"Ha-rry!" My mother practically yelled. "He's an oncologist."

Except he wasn't. Dr. Harry wasn't an oncologist and from what Goth and Edmond had said about his website he'd never claimed to be.

"Now will you stop this, Bobby?"

Looking over at Goth, my dad said, "I'm Jake's dad, Bob." He looked like he was going to try and shake hands but then he didn't. "Which sort of leukemia do you have?"

"I don't. I have cystic fibrosis."

"Oh." He looked a bit confused but recovered quickly, "Well, I hope you do as well as Jake."

"That's Edmond on the other side of the room," I said.

My mom turned and took a peek, but my dad had taken out his phone, studying it intently.

"Is he sleeping?" my mom asked.

"Yeah. He's been sleeping a lot." I said.

My mom nodded. I didn't mind so much that Edmond was sleeping through my parents' visit. I could just imagine him trying to hit on my mom. I didn't need him telling her how much he liked 'cougars.'

"There's no coverage here. I need to call Amelia."

"You called her an hour ago from the car, Bobby. And I've told you a half-dozen times there's no coverage. Why don't you ever believe me?" There was an edge to my mother's voice. An edge that I could imagine ending their marriage.

"There's a jammer," I said.

"Oh, there is not," my mom said. "That's just paranoid. You've seen those maps on TV? None of the cell companies have complete coverage."

"Bad coverage is one or two bars. This is no service. None," my dad pointed out.

"Don't get all conspiracy theory on us. It's simply bad service. That's the America we live in. Everything costs a fortune, and nothing works."

"It's a failure of the entire country?" my father asked. "Why is that more logical than Jake's saying there's a jammer?"

They could have gone on forever, so I jumped in, "Look, there's no wi-fi, there's no cell coverage because they want to keep everything secret until the testing is over. I mean, he cured my leukemia, so there's bound to be other doctors who'd like to get their hands on the cure."

"So, they've done this deliberately?" my dad asked.

"I guess, yeah."

He frowned as though it didn't make sense. And it didn't. Not really. It's not like we were prisoners there. If anyone really wanted to leak secrets, they could just wait until they went home or walk a few hundred feet. I mean, those of us who *could* walk a few hundred feet—Edmond certainly couldn't.

My mom decided to be polite to Goth and ask him a question. "Goliath, where are your parents? Will they be in later?"

"No ma'am. They were glad to see the back of me."

"That can't be true. No parent—"

"I think we should get another opinion," my dad said out of the blue.

"What? Bobby, you can't come here and try to con—"

"Mom stay out of it," I said. She turned and stared at me like I was a stranger. Then I realized I'd probably never told her to stay out of anything. To my dad, I said, "Look, I'm not getting a second opinion. Everything here is fine. I trust Dr. Harry."

Did I trust him? No. Not at all. But I didn't have a choice.

"Can your mother and I meet with Dr. Harry?"

"Jake, that's not a bad idea." Seriously, my mom would have met with my doctors twenty times a day if they let her.

"No," I said, sounding calmer than I was.

My parents stared at me, waiting for me to explain. But I didn't. I wasn't used to taking a stand against them and normally, since they were almost never on the same side, I didn't have to. The whole thing made me nervous, and I felt my heart flip-flop. It stopped, and I held my breath waiting for it to start again. It didn't. Apparently, stress was not good for half-dead hearts.

"That's it?" my mom asked. "Just, no?"

"It's my decision."

Yup, my heart had stopped. I needed to get rid of them and call Dr. Harry.

"This all seems hard to believe, son. It was just a few weeks ago you were getting ready to die, and now it seems like you're not but things don't exactly add up." My dad said, far too rationally. "You're obviously not well. You're getting paler by the moment. It's hard to believe you feel well."

I wasn't paying that much attention. Instead, I was subtly trying to find the call button which was somewhere in my sheets. When he paused, I said, "I feel just fine, Dad."

"Why don't the three of us meet with Dr. Harry?" my mom suggested. My parents were agreeing. That was bizarre. I wanted to lie there and freak out about that, but I really needed to get my heart started again before lividity set in. If my parents were suspicious now, I could imagine what they'd be like if I began to sport big purple spots on half my body. I found the buzzer and started hitting it over and over. "Jake, you're not answering my question."

"No. We're not going to sit down with Dr. Harry as a family. We're not a family."

"Of course, we're a family," my mom said. "Divorce ends a marriage, not a family. We're still your parents, and I know it may not always seem like it, but your father and I do care about each other. We're still partners when it comes to you."

My dad blinked a couple of times. Cheryl Rogers-Margate had not spent a lot of time voicing this opinion. Of course, with my parents agreeing with each other, I felt like I'd taken a trip to opposite world. I glanced over at Goth. He looked at me sympathetically which was humiliating in about six different ways.

Just then, Nurse Kelly came in. "You rang the buzzer?" she asked.

"I need to see Dr. Harry."

"Wait, so we *are* going to meet with him?" my dad asked.

"No. I need to see him *alone*."

"I'm sorry, but Dr. Harry isn't available right now. He asked not to be disturbed."

"I need him, and I need him now. He won't be mad at you."

She looked conflicted. But my mom didn't wait for her to make a decision.

"Jake, what's wrong? You're not feeling well?"

"I just need to see the doctor."

"Is there something I can—" Nurse Kelly started.

"No. I *need* the doctor."

"If you'd explain the problem, this nice young lady is more likely to help you," my dad said.

"The problem is I need to see the doctor."

Goth sat up and put his legs over the side of his bed. From the way he was looking at me, I think he knew exactly what was going on. Well, not exactly but more than anyone else in the room. And more than he should. That wasn't good. I didn't need him figuring out what was happening to me any more than I needed my parents figuring it out.

Nurse Kelly finally decided to get Dr. Harry. My parents got closer to my bed. I had the terrible thought they were about to give me a physical exam to find out why I wanted to see the doctor.

Instead, my mom said, "I don't understand why you suddenly can't trust us. Is it something one of us did?" What she really meant was "did your father do something?"

"No one did anything," I said. "It's just time I take control of my own health."

"Sharing information with us doesn't mean you're not in control, Jake," my dad said.

"We couldn't possibly talk about something else, could we?" I begged.

"What would you like to talk about?"

"How are the halflings and the steplings?"

My dad spent the next few minutes uncomfortably updating me on the doings of the grade school crowd. Then, Dr. Harry hurried onto the ward. Somehow, he managed to look even shabbier than he did the last time I saw him. When he got close to the bed, I said, "I need to see you alone."

"Yes, of course." Clearly, he'd guessed what was happening. He came right to the edge of the bed and helped me out of it.

"Dr. Harry, if possible, Jake's father and I would like to sit down with you for a few minutes before we leave."

"Certainly, as long as it's all right with Jake."

"It's not all right with Jake," I said.

My mom practically growled. "I don't understand why you're being like this."

We were out of the ward and into the reception area, my mom and dad dogging our every step. As Dr. Harry opened the door to the exam room, I gave my parents a stern look and said, "Stay!" as firmly as I could.

I watched the door fall closed on their shocked faces.

thirty-eight

Dr. Harry had to shock me three times before he got my heart going again. By the time he was finished, I felt like I'd been kicked around a corral by a herd of cattle. The burns on my chest were larger and stung, the skin beginning to peel. I noticed Dr. Harry had made sure Nurse Kelly didn't follow us into the examine room, which was good and also bad.

My parents had gone outside and, as I lay on the exam table, I could see them through the blinds having an argument behind my Dad's Lexus hybrid. Behind them, the wind was kicking up whitecaps on the lake. My parents were going to be a problem. I needed them to back off. At least for a while. Once I was stabilized, things would be different.

Dr. Harry put the portable defibrillator away in the cupboard.

"Is this going to keep happening?" I asked. "Will my heart keep stopping like this?"

"We'll find a way to prevent it. There are medications we can try. I already have you on an anti-clotting medication." He stood next to the table. "You should roll over onto your stomach." I did, and he began to massage my back.

"What are you doing?" I asked.

"Rubbing out the bruising," he said. I couldn't believe he used the term 'rubbing out.' He must not know how suggestive that was. Did they not say that when he was young? 'Rubbing one out'?

"So, it's a matter of finding the right medication? To get my heart back on track?"

"Yes. Hopefully."

"And if we don't?"

"I suppose we could implant a pacemaker. But we don't have an operating theater here, and I'm not a surgeon. It would require going to a hospital."

"And that would be difficult," I said, pointing out the obvious.

"Your vital signs would be confusing to most medical professionals."

"I might need a pacemaker to regulate my heart, but I can't get one until we regulate my heart, is that it?"

"It's more complicated than that, but yes. Basically." He lifted the waistband of my pajama bottoms. "Forgive me, but I think I need to massage...your buttocks."

"Oh," I said, remembering that I'd spent a long time in bed with my heart not beating. "Um... Nobody's going see that part of me."

"We're trying to keep the blood flowing."

"Okay, yeah, go ahead."

I tried not to think about what he was doing. It was pretty embarrassing. It was also kind of relaxing, though. At least the part where he massaged my back. I drifted a bit, then asked, "What about the stem cell treatment? That will help, won't it?"

"I still have hopes for that. Your other organ systems seem to be improving. Your urine output is almost normal. Is your appetite improving?"

"Yes," I lied.

"Good. I think everything should even out in a week or two. How are you getting on with Goliath?"

"Why are you asking me that?"

"Is there a reason I shouldn't ask you?"

"You knew Goth and I were gay when you chose us, didn't you?"

"Goth told me his story, yes. And your mother told me yours."

"You didn't want me to be dead alone."

"Please don't think of yourself as dead. That's not productive. And it's not true."

"Other people would think of me that way."

"You redefine the meaning of death."

Even if I'd had time to come up with goals before I got sick, I was pretty sure redefining the meaning of death would not have been among them. College. Boyfriend. Interesting career, probably. See, no redefining death.

thirty-nine

Clattering. Chattering. The sounds of dishes clanking together and people talking. A restaurant. I barely understood where I was. Or wasn't. The restaurant was once a simple two-story house, so the rooms are small. Their table was in the part of the house that was once the front porch.

"Why do you think Jake needed to see the doctor so badly?"

"I don't know, Bobby. He may not have needed to see the doctor. He might have just been asserting his independence."

"Really? That's what you think?"

"Yes, that's what I think."

"Well, what do you think about this new independent streak?" my father asked, buttering a piece of bread.

"I'm not sure we can complain about it. I mean, it's a normal part of growing up."

"I'll complain about it. Look, I know he's almost twenty and should be making his own decisions, but I feel like he's completely cutting us out. If he were a healthy kid out on his own, all right. But he's not."

"I do trust Dr. Harry."

My mother sipped her glass of red wine.

"I might trust him, too, if I got to sit down and talk to him."

"We'll try again tomorrow."

"And I want to be able to communicate with Jake during the week. It's

ridiculous that they're blocking phone reception and wi-fi. It's not the CIA. They're not guarding national secrets."

"Don't take it so personally, Bobby. It's not directed at you."

The look on my dad's face said he was resisting the temptation to snap at her. I could practically see him biting his tongue.

"Well, maybe when they get more patients. Speaking of which, why aren't there more patients?"

"They're not patients. They're research subjects. And, now that Jake is a success, I'm sure they'll fill the place up."

"Oh my God, how new is this treatment? I know you say he's better, but if it's all experimental that means anything could—"

"Our son would be dead right now if he hadn't come. We both know that."

He couldn't say anything to that.

"Look, Jake wants to be here. He wouldn't have agreed if he wasn't willing to take chances, and it's too late to second guess his decision." That made it sound like I'd actually agreed to come, which I didn't remember doing. I didn't remember making a decision, exactly.

"Cher, I appreciate your saying that we're still a family. That we're partners when it comes to Jake."

"Well, we are..." She stopped and frowned. "I know I may have struggled with that from time to time. But I have always been glad you've stayed in Jake's life."

"Me too."

The waitress arrived with their lunch order and set the dishes down in front of them. My mom and dad gave each other an uncomfortable look and then began eating.

"Be careful what you say." It was Dr. Harry's voice. But why was he at dinner with my parents?

He wasn't. He was in his office, talking into his computer screen.

"Someone may be listening in."

In a window on Dr. Harry's screen, Dr. Callabray stared out. "Why would someone—? Have you been hacked? I thought your location was secure?"

"It is. There has been a development. The subject has developed abilities which seem to be unscientific."

"Dr. Harry, have you been getting enough sleep?"

"Of course I haven't been getting enough sleep, but that has nothing to do with the things I've observed. The subject has heightened hearing for one thing..."

"Really?" Dr. Callabray seemed to consider. "There have been reports of heightened senses surrounding death. Have you done any testing?"

"No. I'm not sure I want him to understand the extent of his abilities."

"You said 'for one thing.' There's more?"

"He claims he's able to project his consciousness outside of his body and he knows things he shouldn't know."

"I'm sure that's more coincidence than anything else."

"He's seen things in my office, but there's no way he could have been in there. I keep it locked."

"He could be guessing. Or maybe you're wrong. Maybe he was in there." There was a stern look on his face. "You know what you're talking about isn't possible scientifically. You're talking about metaphysics. That's not science."

"I can only report the data I'm seeing."

"This is all very disappointing. I'd hoped you were calling about another matter."

Dr. Harry took a moment. I could tell he didn't want to say what he was about to say. "You'll be happy to know I've had a change of heart. I'll be moving forward with five new subjects."

"You will? Well, that's good to hear," Dr. Callabray said. "Can I ask what changed your mind?"

"I've gone over the test results again, and I find that they're more encouraging than I originally thought."

"Excellent. You didn't happen to get a letter from my attorney, did you?"

"No, I didn't."

"If you do, just ignore it." Dr. Callabray looked uncomfortable for a moment. "I hope you understand that having investors involved changes, well, everything. The potential earnings from Property Five and the supportive treatment we're developing are simply massive. We have a duty to do everything we can to bring it to market."

"Yes, Dr. Callabray, I understand our duty." Dr. Harry smiled at his computer screen. He wasn't very good at smiling. "We'll move forward as quickly as we can."

"I'm so glad to hear it," Dr. Callabray said.

And so was I.

forty

I woke to the sound of giggling girls, and I was giddy.

It was Saturday evening, already dark. I glanced out the window, through the fly-spotted screen. The sun had set while I slept. Dr. Harry was going to continue with the study. Things were going to get better. Goth wouldn't die. Neither would Edmond or the giggling girls.

Wrestling myself into a sitting position, I looked across the ward and saw three girls, two of whom were bald, hanging out on Edmond's bed. The center of attention, Edmond looked like he'd died and gone to heaven.

"Look, he's awake," Edmond said. "This is my friend, Jake."

I wondered when exactly we became friends but smiled at them all anyway.

"This is Rochelle and Cammy and Lea," Edmond continued.

Lea was the girl closest to him. She was thin and tall and wore a red scarf tied tight around her head. She had a blush in her cheeks that made her look almost healthy. Edmond couldn't take his eyes off her. And, surprisingly, she looked back at him with the same fervor. Were they really in love? I hated to think they were. They'd just met, after all, but it looked like love. It did. Maybe it was only the hope love would happen. The hope they'd live long enough to fall in love for real.

I wondered if this is what I was feeling for Goth. Hope instead of love.

I mean, I hadn't actually thought of my feelings for him as love. Not exactly. They were probably more lust. Was lust a sort of hope? And was it likely those feelings would turn to love? I was going to be around for a long while, so I guess I didn't have to hurry through things. I had time to feel my way through this.

"I saw this thing on the Internet," Edmond said breathlessly. Well, everything he said was a bit breathless. "Did you know that you can't grow beans from the beans you get in the supermarket?"

The girls looked at him in awe.

"I doubt that's true," Goth said.

"No, it is. If you want to grow anything, you have to send away and pay a copyright fee."

Goth looked at me and rolled his eyes.

"I mean, think about it," Edmond continued. "What if there's an apocalypse? Nobody will be able to grow beans. No one will be able to grow any kind of food. As soon as the canned food is gone, everyone will starve."

I guess that was Edmond for you. Sick with a deadly disease but concerned about how to get food during the coming apocalypse.

The girl named Cammy had come over to my bed and stood staring at me. She was the one who still had hair, though it looked more like steel wool. The way she looked at me was kind of creepy.

"My brother's gay. He's my favorite person in the world." I had the uncomfortable feeling I'd already been nominated for second favorite. I wasn't thrilled.

"Okay," I said, because what else do you say to something like that?

"He's a radical. He thinks the whole gay marriage thing was just a waste of time. Marriage is stupid. He hates that gays are getting married and having all these babies. He thinks they ought to be having sex all the time because that, because..." She paused. Obviously, she'd forgotten why her brother thought gay guys should be having sex all the time. "Well...just because. What do you think?"

I looked over at Goth who lay in his bed smirking. I raised my eyebrows in a very clear SOS, which he ignored.

"Um, how old are you?" I asked.

"Almost seventeen."

"I think maybe you should wait a few years before you have conversations like this." Forming a philosophy about the sexual behavior of gay men hardly seemed imperative for a sixteen-year-old girl.

"But I might not be here in a few years," Cammy replied as though I was completely idiotic. "I have non-Hodgkin's lymphoma, which is totally stupid."

"Yeah, cancer is stupid," I said, deciding to be agreeable.

"No, I mean the name." She rolled her eyes. Clearly, I was an idiot. "Telling people what kind of cancer you have by telling them what kind of cancer you don't have. It's just stupid. The recovery rate for my cancer is ninety percent."

"Oh. That's good. So why are you here?"

Another eye roll. "Somebody has to be in the ten percent. My brother says it's because I'm special. Being special isn't as cool as he thinks it is."

"No, I guess not."

"You're the one who got cured, aren't you?"

"Yeah, I guess."

She studied me closely. "You don't look very good."

"Thanks."

She shrugged. "People who aren't sick anymore shouldn't look sick."

"There's this thing called small talk, have you ever heard of it?"

She frowned at me. "I know what small talk is. It's boring. If I get cured, I'm going to look better than you."

I didn't have time to come up with a response because Rochelle said very loudly, "Oh! That is just disgusting." I glanced over to see Lea pulling her hand out from under the sheet on Edmond's bed. Edmond had a rapturous look on his face.

"Oh my God, she did it," Rochelle called across the room to Cammy. "She said she was going to give him a handie and she did."

"That is so gross!" Cammy nearly shouted. It seemed her philosophy on the sexual behavior of teenage girls was fully formed. She was clearly against.

"She just touched it a little," Edmond said, obviously wanting to defend Lea but not doing such a great job.

After that, it was downhill. Cammy and Rochelle insisted that it was time to go back to the ward. When Lea tried to stay, they refused to leave without her. So, after a bit of haggling, all three girls left.

forty-one

I slept like the dead that night, which I suppose should not come as a surprise. Twelve hours. Maybe thirteen. I was out. When I finally woke, my parents were standing at the foot of my bed. My mom had a piece of cheesecake for me. I took a few bites, and it was completely disgusting. Everything I ate was disgusting. I had this horrible thought that my taste buds had decomposed to the point where I'd never enjoy eating again.

It was a sucky thought.

But then I remembered Dr. Harry had looked at the data again and was encouraged. I wanted to see him and ask him when he was going to start giving the others Property Five. First, though, I had to spend the day with my parents.

They took me out to the solarium to visit. It was a hot day and insects were buzzing outside. My dad was wearing shorts and sweating; my mom looked comfortable in a sundress and flip-flops. Sunlight seemed to be everywhere, and I squinted at my dad as he talked about how he wanted to corner Dr. Harry and insist that he provide wi-fi.

The way he was talking, you'd think an Internet connection was now a constitutional right. When I said that might not be a good idea, that Dr. Harry had plenty do with without turning the Institute into a Starbucks, he offered to pay for the wireless.

"That's an important life lesson, Jake. When you offer people shit for free, they rarely turn it down."

I just nodded when he said that. It might be true, but I had the feeling there were more important life lessons I needed to learn. Surprisingly, it was my mom who came to my rescue. Out of the blue, she said, "Bobby, we may be taking this all the wrong way. If Jake wants to be more independent, it's because he's getting better. This is exactly what we've always hoped for. That he'd get better, that he'd be able to grow up."

My dad looked at me, then at her, then back at me, and asked, "This is you growing up?"

"Yes," I said. It was way better than the truth, so I was going to latch onto it as hard as I could. "I'm growing up."

"Don't feel like you have to grow up entirely. Your mom and I like it when you need us. Separately or together. Either way."

That made me feel sort of bad. My parents were both pretty decent, even if they were really annoying, and the fact that I was lying to them made me feel shitty. I mean, I hadn't been in any big rush to tell them I was gay, but that was different. They didn't *need* to know that. They did kind of *need* to know that—in certain circles at least—I was dead. Or kind of dead. They were going to be really pissed when they found out.

I coaxed my mom into talking about how her week at work was. They were super happy to have her back, and she glowed a little while talking about the things her boss—

Someone was screaming in my ward. It was Goth. He was yelling for help. I rushed out of the solarium, down the hall to the ward. My parents came behind me. When I got into the ward, the first thing I saw was Nurse Kelly on top of Edmond pumping his chest.

"He's not breathing," Goth yelled. "We need Dr. Harry. Where's Dr. Harry?"

"He's upstairs," Nurse Kelly said, pumping on Edmond's chest.

I rushed out of the ward, through the reception area and up the stairs. I got to the landing and had to stop. I hadn't moved this quickly in years. I huffed and puffed, looking at the resurrected Jesus as I caught my breath. Even in stained glass, you could tell he was Anglo-Jesus. Almost blond. Blue eyes. Very white skin today. The look on his face was pity. He was sorry for those he'd left on earth, sorry for the living.

Pushing on to the second floor, I began to shout Dr. Harry's name. I knew where his office wasn't. It wasn't to my right, because that was the Ray's room with the scanner, and it wasn't either of the two doors just to my left I'd been in—

He came out of the door farthest from the stairs on the left. Almost directly above my bed. He'd heard me yelling.

"It's Edmond. He's dying."

He started to rush by me. I grabbed at his arm. "Wait. Don't you have to get Property Five?"

"I can't. It would be unethical."

"What? No, you're going to give everyone Property Five. Just give it to Edmond now. You told—" He seemed to recoil from me, and that's when I knew he'd lied. That he'd lied to Dr. Callabray and, because I'd been eavesdropping, lied to me. "Edmond will die."

"Let me at least see if I can help him." He ran away from me and down the stairs.

Why was it unethical to give Edmond Property Five when it had been ethical to give it to me? He was dying. Right that minute he was dying. What was ethical about letting him die?

I hurried after Dr. Harry, down the stairs and into the ward. My parents were pressed together at the foot of my bed. Nurse Kelly and Dr. Harry were standing around Edmond's bed. They weren't doing a thing. Just standing. Looking at him. He was very still. His eyes open. Flat. Dead. He was gone.

I slipped up behind Dr. Harry and asked, "Can you still give it to him?"

"There's nothing we can do. He's gone."

"But there is—"

"Be quiet, Jake." His voice was hard-edged and sharp. He stared at me with such power, I actually wondered what he might do to me.

He'd done the wrong thing. That's what Dr. Harry thought. He'd done the wrong thing giving me Property Five. Did that mean I was just like his other failed experiments? That he was going to hide me, chop me into little pieces? No, he couldn't do that. I was still here, alive or sort of alive. Alive-ish.

And wasn't that better than being actually, really dead?

forty-two

It came as a complete surprise to me that it was Labor Day weekend. After Edmond died, while he lay there under a sheet and we all kind of wondered what exactly we were supposed to do while a dead man was in the room, I asked my parents what time they were leaving.

"We're not leaving until tomorrow, dear," my mom said.

"What?"

"It's a holiday weekend."

"Oh. And you're spending it all here?"

"Amelia took the twins to her parents for the weekend, and Kevin and Kourtney are with their father." My dad said, explaining why the steplings and halflings could do without him for three whole days. My mom didn't have to explain anything. I was it for her.

"Are you all right, Jake?" she asked for about the sixth time in an hour.

I wasn't, but if I said I wasn't, I'd have to explain. My mom thought explanations solved everything. I didn't agree. "Yeah, I'm okay."

"The way you ran out of the ward, Jake, that's the first time I really believed you were getting better," my dad said.

"Thanks for the vote of confidence, Bobby. I've been telling you he's better for weeks."

"I'm sorry. I should have believed you." He looked at me intently and asked, "Jake, what were you saying to Dr. Harry? You wanted him to give that boy something?"

"Oh, I don't think you heard right," my mom interrupted. "He just wanted the doctor to do something to save the poor boy. That's what we all wanted."

I looked at her, but she wouldn't look back at me. It seemed like she didn't want my dad asking questions about Property Five. I wondered how much she knew about what it actually—

"Is there something Dr. Harry could have done that he didn't do?" my dad asked, ignoring what my mom had said.

"No. I was wrong. I thought there was, but I was wrong."

"Exactly what kind of drug did he give you, Jake?"

"Bobby, he's upset. You need to leave him alone. We watched a boy die." She kept her voice low, as though Edmond might hear us.

We were silent for a bit. The best thing families could be sometimes was silent. Outside, it was a lovely fall day, temperate and bright. The prettiness of the day seemed to clash with Edmond's death. How could people die on a lovely afternoon? Death was darkness, night, stormy days with thunder. No one should die beneath a bright blue, cloudless sky.

Looking out the window, I watched as a black panel van pulled to a stop in front of the Institute. On the side, in gold lettering, it said HEARTWELL MORTUARY. There was a contradiction in terms. If your heart was well you certainly didn't need a mortuary. I wondered if they got more business by naming themselves what they obviously were not.

A few minutes later, an older, fussy guy in a gray suit walked into the ward. Behind him a kid, who had the same reptilian look Ray had, pushed a gurney. They set about moving Edmond from the bed to the gurney.

"Don't you usually need to call the police when someone dies?" my dad whispered.

"Not if someone dies in the hospital," my mom explained.

"You said this wasn't a hospital. You said it's a research—"

"Medical facility, then. Really Bobby, I think everyone here knows what they're doing." That was a funny thing for her to say. I mean, a lot of the people at The Godwin Institute didn't seem to know what they were doing at all. And she knew that. Then she said, "His poor parents."

"Yeah," my dad said. They looked at each other for a moment. Clearly, it could have been me being rolled out of the Institute on a gurney. Then, to try and turn the mood—obviously—my dad said, "I think we should ask Dr. Harry if we can take Jake on a field trip. Into town for lunch. Or just an ice cream."

"Oh, they have wonderful ice cream up here. I had some. Jake you'll love it. Sweet vanilla with tart cherries."

No way was I going on a field trip with them. For one thing, my heart might stop, and I needed to be near Dr. Harry and the defibrillator—which sounds like some kind of perverted children's book if you ask me—plus, if all they could think of to do was go someplace and eat, that was going to be a drag. I mean, they'd probably notice if I ordered lunch and then barely ate any of it. And if they noticed, they wouldn't leave me alone about it.

"I'm fine here. But you guys go if you want."

My dad looked at me funny. "Jake, we're here to spend time with you. It's the whole point."

"Yeah, I know." I had to throw them a bone. "The lake is right across the street. Maybe we can walk out there."

"And have a picnic!" my mom immediately added.

I was doomed.

forty-three

Sex, as it turns out, is not like porn. Not that I've seen a lot of porn, I mean my mom did go to work every day and leave me alone for years, so I have seen some, but the whole I'm-a-dying-teenager was also a natural boner killer—as was the fact that I had to constantly erase my browser history. Anyway, sex with Goth wasn't anything like porn. It was like air. Like being able to breathe for the first time in a long time. I wondered how I'd ever lived without it.

Both my parents had a much better appetite than I did and eventually they left to have dinner. My dinner came. Fried rice. Everyone had Chinese food that night. The nice thing about it was that I could move it around on my plate and no one could really be sure how little I actually ate.

After dinner, Goth took off his cannula and climbed into bed with me. He had his portable DVD player and flipped on an old black and white Hitchcock movie about a happy family that doesn't stay that way. We didn't really watch the movie, though.

"Can I have your fortune cookie?" Goth asked as the opening credits rolled. I gave it to him, and he ate it quickly then read the little strip of paper that had been inside, "Your future is so bright you have to wear sunglasses." He giggled.

Then a few moments later he said, "Sucks about Edmond."

"It does."

"I mean, it's not like we knew him very well, but, man, dying like that."

He stared at the DVD player without looking at it. I thought I saw tears welling in his eyes.

"Totally sucks." I said. Eloquent, I know.

"I heard what you said to Dr. Harry. You're mad at him for not giving Edmond the treatment."

"No. I mean, kind of. I get that it's a study, and you have to follow certain rules. But he was dying. He did die."

"Does it work that fast, though? I mean, you just give it to someone, and they're instantly cured?"

"Sort of."

"Then he should have given it to Edmond. I don't understand why he wouldn't."

"Dr. Harry's not big on explaining his reasons for why he does shit, is he?"

"No, he's not."

I felt bad about not telling Goth the truth, but I wasn't exactly sure whether it was a good idea or a bad one. We watched the movie for a minute. There were some jokes in it about using the telephone. They acted like it was a relatively recent invention. Goth whispered into my ear, "It should be tonight."

"What should be tonight?"

"You and me. Us. The end of the virgins. I mean, who knows what's going to happen next, right? We may never have another chance."

"Aren't you sick?"

"I'll be less sick over here."

"You want to do it here? What about Miss Haggerty?"

"At midnight, she takes a serious, snoring nap. It lasts about two hours." He leaned forward on his bed and whispered. I hadn't put two and two together. Of course, she took a nap every night. She was stealing morphine. It wasn't likely to keep her awake. "That's when we could do it. Set your alarm."

I went to the clock app on my iPad and set the alarm to vibrate at twelve-thirty. Now we just had to wait six hours. Six long hours.

"What if she wakes up?" She probably wouldn't but still.

"She won't. And even if she does, we just need to be quiet enough that she doesn't turn around."

"So you've really never done this before? You're pretty good at it."

"Natural affinity. I was homeschooled, so the only time I ever saw anyone was at church and the pickings were slim. You really a virgin? Or have you just been stringing me along?"

"Trust me. You're going to find out I have no idea what I'm doing."

That made him laugh.

Dinner came. That night they brought Goth a mini-pizza. I tried to be jealous while I worked my way up through half a can of chicken soup and a few bites of rice pudding. Then we watched one of the three movies I had on my iPad, the really gruesome one that no one ever admits to watching, about piranhas eating sexy coeds. I don't even want to say the name it's so embarrassing.

Anyway, about halfway through, right after the part where the annoying TV reporter stands in the lake to report on the dead coeds and doesn't even notice when his feet are put on the piranha lunch program, Goth said, "Hey, you got your wish."

"What wish?"

"You wanted to lose your virginity after a romantic dinner and a movie."

I remembered we talked about sex and romance when we first met. I was pretty sure he was the one who'd mentioned dinner and a movie. But it didn't matter. He was right. This was my wish. This was how I wanted things to be. Or at least it was as close as we could come given our current circumstances.

"Yeah, you're right. This is romantic." I nuzzled him and kissed his neck. I didn't dare do much more since Miss Haggerty, who'd started work right after dinner, could turn around and watch us if she felt like it. Her naptime still a couple hours away.

We finished the movie a few minutes before lights out at ten. Of course, I couldn't fall asleep, and from the rustling coming from Goth's bed, he couldn't either. Two and a half hours when you're waiting for something you really want feels as long as three weeks, maybe four. A month. It felt like I waited a month for my alarm to go off. Miss Haggerty had been asleep for about twenty minutes—I'd been stealing peeks at my iPad under the blanket, keeping track of time's crawl. I wanted to jump the gun and crawl into Goth's bed the second I saw Miss Haggerty's head tip forward onto her chest, but I waited because I didn't want her waking up. Goth might not be worried about it, but I was.

I turned the alarm off before it had time to vibrate, my heart beating hard in my chest. A good sign for me. I hoped it wouldn't stop while we were "doing it." That sometimes happened to people, mostly old guys on top of really young women. Of course, if it did happen to me, I wouldn't actually have to stop having sex.

I quietly got out of bed and crept across the few feet between our beds. I climbed in with Goth. He seemed to be wide awake, too. He slipped his arms around me and whispered into my ear. "Hey, bae. You sleep? I didn't."

I shook my head and kissed him. His lips, his scalding lips. And his mouth like an oven. Every time I kissed him, it was as though he was breathing life into me. I wondered if kissing Goth might be better for me than anything Dr. Harry could invent. Could Goth bring me back to life, real life, with just his kisses? I wished it could happen, but I knew it couldn't.

We stopped kissing and unbuttoned each other's pajama tops. He pulled me close so that we were skin to skin. He was warm and soft, like slipping into a bath. I worried about what he might be feeling, though. "I'm not too cold, am I?"

"No. I like it."

A moment later, we were wiggling out of our pajama bottoms. Luckily, at that particular moment, my blood was flowing pretty well, and I didn't have to be embarrassed by anything, you know, not happening. The rest of me, though. Man. There were red, peeling spots on my chest from being shocked and cuts on my feet from walking barefoot outside. I smelled. And in the right light, I looked green.

Yeah, I was sex on a stick.

"How can you want to have sex with me?" I asked. "I'm coming apart."

"How can you want to have sex with me? I'm dying."

"But you're beautiful."

"And so are you."

He took me into his hand and put my hand on him. We rubbed each other while we kissed. His hands were nearly as hot as his lips. Part of me wanted to do nothing but lay back and feel his warmth, while another part wanted to run my cool hands over him like a mountain stream.

What we were doing wasn't all that different from what we'd done to ourselves when we were alone, and it wasn't going to be enough for either of us. Goth pulled the blanket over his head and wiggled down, licking my belly as he went.

When he reached his destination, it felt so good I groaned. Then I was instantly terrified I'd been too loud. Goth must have worried about it, too, since he stopped. We listened, but Miss Haggerty didn't come storming into the ward to see what was happening. After a moment, Goth began to move again, taking me to a gasping, shivering place.

A moment later, he crawled back up the bed and lay next to me. His breath came in short, thin pants. He pulled me on top of him, and in a breathy whisper said, "I'm sorry. You're going to have to do most of the work."

I nodded and began to move down his belly, but he stopped me. "No. I want you inside me."

"Really?"

"There's some lotion in the nightstand."

I leaned over and opened the drawer. Inside was a small tube of hand lotion. I felt around for something else, but all I found was the lotion. "Don't we need, you know, protection?"

"Seriously? We're both virgins. And even if you're lying to me and you aren't, well...it would be a luxury to live long enough to die of something else."

"I don't want to think about that."

"Then don't. I'm right here. And I want you. Think about that."

I kept my eyes on him as I got us ready. When I was about to enter him, he said, "Keep your eyes on mine. Look into my heart."

And that's what I did. Inside, he was even warmer than he was outside and I couldn't help but feel I was making love to fire. That we were fire and ice. Except neither would give an inch. I couldn't smother him any more than he could melt me. We were fixed. Permanent.

His eyes were dark, earthen brown, expressive. Every push, every thrust was reflected in his eyes. At first, I saw tension, even pain, but then it gave way to pleasure, lust, connection, love. And I felt it, felt his love. It wasn't like I'd never been loved before. My parents loved me. My mother loved me to the point of insanity. But this was different. My parents would have loved whatever child they had. Goth loved me because I was me. I wasn't sure anyone ever would again.

He clung to me.

"This is okay?" I asked.

"You're better at this than you thought you'd be."

I kissed him in response, then in a spasm that felt like a dam breaking, flooding, releasing, I came. And Goth a moment later. We stopped, shivering when we pulled apart as though separating chilled us both.

"I love you," he whispered.

"I know. I saw it in your eyes. I love you, too."

"Thank you."

"Thank you? That's so weird, why are you thanking me?"

"Bucket list. I didn't want to die without saying 'I love you' to the right guy."

I couldn't help thinking that I'd had to die in order to find someone to love. I didn't say it, though. It didn't seem the right time to talk about being dead. Not to mention, I didn't feel dead. Not when I was with Goth.

We held each other and drifted. Eventually, I fell asleep.

forty-four

While we were going through our routine the next morning, Goth and I kept peeking at each other and trying not to giggle. Nurse Kelly noticed how we were acting and eyed us suspiciously.

"What's the joke?" she asked.

"Nothing," I said.

"Sometimes it's just nice to be alive," Goth said.

"Do you still need the oxygen?" she asked, as though to challenge him.

He stopped smiling. "Yeah, I do."

That gave me a sinking feeling. I guess that was something else I was learning about sex. It made you forget all the shitty things that were happening. I hadn't thought about Goth being sick in almost a whole day.

Nurse Kelly fitted Goth up with the cannula and checked the levels on the oxygen. "You'll need a new tank soon. I'll be back in a few minutes."

When she left, I asked him, "So you're not feeling better." Then I nearly bit my tongue off. "You know what? Don't answer. I've been getting asked that for five years and I hated it. Usually I lied."

Goth shrugged. "I'm not feeling much better physically. Emotionally, I feel amazing."

That made me smile. I wanted to go over and crawl into bed with him but knew I'd have to wait until it was dark, and Miss Haggerty took her morphine nap. I wondered if I should tell Goth about the dreaming, sleepwalking thing I did—not yet, though. Eventually, but not now. Now I wanted to enjoy the fact that he really liked me. Loved me. Which would be easier to do if he wasn't wondering if I was batshit crazy.

What if Goth got sicker? What if Dr. Harry wouldn't give him Property—

My parents walked in. My dad had his arms full of two brown paper bags. He said, "Come on, Jake. We're going to have brunch on the beach. Then your mom and I have to get on the road. We have to be back in Chicago."

"*You* have to get back to Chicago. I'm just a passenger," my mother pointed out, but she didn't seem so upset about going home.

"I'm sorry, Cher, I am. It's not my fault." To me, he said, "Kevin and Kourtney—"

"The steplings," I corrected, so that Goth would be able to follow the conversation. When I glanced over at him, he was practically smirking.

"Yes, the steplings. Their dad was supposed to keep them until tomorrow morning, but he's dropping them off this afternoon. And Amelia's not going to be home with the twins until eight tonight."

"They're teenagers. They can't be alone for a few hours?" I don't know why I said that. I actually wanted my parents to leave so I could spend the whole day with Goth. What I'd meant was "Bye-bye!"

"Listen to what you just said, Jake. Teenagers. Alone. Hours. Not a good idea."

"Yeah, I guess."

After that, I couldn't do much but let them drag me out of bed. Stealing glances at Goth as we left, I hoped maybe he'd take a nap while we were gone and feel amazingly better when I got back. My parents walked me out of the ward, out of the building, then down the walk to the street and across to the small beach.

There was a straggly tree on one side and a well-weathered pile of firewood that could be used to make a bonfire. My mom spread a blanket across the sand. My dad carried it in the back of his car, just in case. My mom traveled with thick towels, and my dad traveled with a blanket. They were a lot more alike than they'd ever admit.

"Do we have any idea how long you're going to be here, Jake?" my dad asked. He probably wanted to know if he'd have to come back. Less than a month, he wouldn't have to. More than a month, and he might feel obligated.

"We don't," my mom said before I could answer. "It's research, so it's important."

"I didn't say it wasn't important. I just want to know how long my son's going to be here." My dad was starting to unpack the bags. "And I'm sure they're going to be studying Jake even after he leaves."

My mom decided to ignore him. "Jake, we got all your favorites at the deli. Ham and Swiss on a Kaiser roll. Mayo, mustard, relish. Smashed potato salad. Coleslaw. And that fruit salad you like, ambrosia."

My favorites? It was news to me. Not to mention I was about as far from hungry as you could get. "I just had a big breakfast."

"You did? What did you eat?"

"Eggs and bacon and a couple of pancakes." That was Goth's breakfast from Mickey D's. My real breakfast was a few bites of oatmeal and a spoonful of yogurt that I'd been tempted to spit out.

"Good. You're getting your appetite back," my mother said. "I'm sure you can find a little room for brunch."

My dad was spreading everything out on the blanket. They'd thought of everything. Paper plates, plastic forks, little packets of mustard for the sandwiches. I stood, reluctant to sit down. I was a little worried that the ants might choose me over the picnic. I'd already attracted one fly, which I swatted at a couple of times.

Part of me wanted to tell them I wasn't a virgin anymore, that I was head-over-heels in love with Goth, but that would make the whole brunch even weirder than it already was. I mean, I hadn't officially told my dad I was gay. He'd be cool. My mom would be gushy which would be decidedly uncool. Still, I'd never thought it would happen so I kind of—

"Jake, you're smiling. You really are feeling better, aren't you?"

"I bought champagne," my dad announced, pulling a bottle out of the bag. "We should celebrate your getting better."

"But I'm not twenty-one."

"Oh, my God, what kind of child did we raise?" he said to my mom.

"You can have a glass of champagne with your parents, Jake. No one will arrest you."

My mom made a plate of food for me, piling it ridiculously high on the plate. She set it in front of me, and I ignored it. When we each had a plastic cup of champagne, my dad proposed a toast. "To Jake, who has a future."

We clinked glasses but not really. Plastic glasses don't clink. They don't make much of a sound at all.

I took a sip of champagne. It tasted sharp and kind of sour. One sip was enough, I set the glass down on the blanket and ignored it. I kind of hoped it would spill so I didn't have to drink it.

Reluctantly, I picked up the plastic fork and scooped up some ambrosia. It didn't look appealing, but my mom would be all over me if I didn't at least try to eat. I got it in my mouth and chewed on it for a long time.

"Jake, you should really get a timeline from Dr. Harry," my dad suggested. Back to topic. "That way we can talk about getting you into school for the spring semester."

My mom had said things like that herself but now she was silent. Just sipping her champagne instead.

"I haven't thought about it much," I said. "A lot has happened in the last few weeks."

"Why don't we put our feet into the lake?" my mom suggested.

I looked out at the lake, which was choppy and angry looking. "Isn't it awfully cold?" Not that I would notice that.

"It might be. It has been a very cold summer."

"Cher, it's one of the hottest summers on record."

"Oh, it is not."

"It is. Google it." Suddenly, the phone in his pocket pinged. He pulled it out and looked at it. "Huh, I got a text. From Amelia."

He typed in a quick text and then waited. "Crap, it's not going through. I've barely got a bar." He stood up and, holding the phone up in the air, tried to find a better signal. "I'll be right back," he said, wandering off down the beach.

"Your friend Goliath didn't look very good today."

"He'll be okay."

"Of course, he'll be okay. Dr. Harry knows what he's doing."

Did he? He wasn't happy with the way things were going. So unhappy that he wouldn't give Edmund the treatment even though he was dying. Property Five worked, but everything after it didn't. That meant Dr. Harry didn't really know what he was doing at all.

"Why do you believe in him?" I asked.

"Jake, he saved you. And you're doing so well."

An idea had been slowly forming in my head for a while. Suddenly it popped. Became whole and I realized... "You knew, didn't you? You've known all along?"

"Known what?"

"That Dr. Harry wasn't an oncologist. That the treatment I'm getting isn't for leukemia."

"Of course the treatment was for leukemia. You're cured, aren't you?"

"Tell the truth, Mom. You told Dad that Dr. Harry was an oncologist, but you saw his website. You were communicating with him before we came. You knew he wasn't an oncologist. You knew he was studying life extension. Not leukemia."

"Life is life, Jake. He said he could save you. That's all I needed to know."

"But I wasn't saved. I was just— I'm a different kind of sick now. That's all. A sick that isn't ever going to end."

"I have every confidence that, Dr. Harry—"

"Edmond died. Dr. Harry decided not to give him Property Five because of me, because I'm not doing as well as he'd like."

"That's not true, Jake. You've misunderstood the situation. I'll have a talk—"

"I've been using that cologne you gave me—"

"Oh, good—"

"But I still smell bad. And it's not because I'm not bathing properly. I smell because I'm decomposing."

"Decomposing? Oh, that is so overly dramatic." She chuckled. "You know, I don't think any woman is really prepared to raise a boy. The things that interest you are so alien. I mean, literally aliens sometimes. And zombies. And vampires. And violent. Everything boys think about is so violent. Even with your being gay it's still about these creepy, weird—"

"Mom, the night I got here. I died."

"You had a close call. But you were saved."

"I died. And Dr. Harry couldn't bring me back."

She frowned, lines bracketing her mouth. "So, are you a ghost? Is that what you're saying?"

"No. I'm not a ghost. But I'm not alive."

"You're sitting right there. Talking to me. You're alive."

I shook my head. "No, you're wrong. I'm conscious. It's not the same thing as alive. Not anymore."

"Jake, you're not dead, so you have to be alive."

"I'm something else. Something in between. Something very wrong."

"Morbid. That's the thing about boys. No matter what they have this disturbing morbid streak that is so—"

"STOP IT! STOP PRETENDING!"

She breathed heavily for a moment, glanced down the beach at my father who looked to have gotten enough bars and had made a call. After a deep cleansing breath, she said, "You don't understand, Jake. I'm not sure you can. You don't know what it's like, a mother's love for her son. It's everything. I love you. I love you too much to let you die. I had to do everything I could. Whatever it was, I had to do it. And I'd do it again. In a heartbeat. I hope, maybe, someday you'll love someone enough to understand what I did."

We stared at each other. Did I understand what she was saying? I didn't know. It seemed really big. But I did know I couldn't tell her to stop loving me. It would be kind of pointless.

Then she said, "Jake, there's something crawling out of your ear."

And just as she said it, I could feel it. I reached up and swiped my ear with my finger. When I looked at my hand there were a half dozen, cream-colored pieces of rice lying there; rice that wiggled.

forty-five

Maggots. Maggots were crawling out of my ear.

"Oh my God," Nurse Kelly said. The way she looked at me suggested no one in nursing school had mentioned she might have to deal with something this gross. "I'll get Dr. Harry."

My parents were flipping out. Well, my dad was. Whatever was going on with Amelia and the steplings, it was now even more important that my parents get on the road. But here I was having another medical crisis. I could tell he really wanted to ask how long it was all going to take but was afraid it would be obnoxious.

"You guys can go if you need to."

"No, Jake, we need to stay," my mom said.

"To do what?" I asked. "Dr. Harry will be here in a minute, and we'll go into the exam room. And you'll wait out here. I don't need you to do that."

"He does have a point, Cher."

My mom looked at me closely. I could tell she was thinking about our conversation. That maybe it would be good if she left and gave me a little time. "Are you sure, Jake?"

"I'm sure."

"All right then," my dad said. He stepped forward and hugged me. He frowned at the smell of me but didn't say anything.

My mom hugged me. "I'll be back on Friday," she said. And then pulled me down to whisper into my ear. "I hope you can forgive me." She stepped back, waiting for me to say I forgave her.

But I couldn't say it. Not yet.

Dr. Harry rushed down the stairs, looking as though he hadn't slept in a week. His face was sallow, his cheeks sunken and grisly. His beard was still a mess. It looked like he'd tried to clean up his neck but only succeeded in slicing his Adam's apple.

His eyes flashed to my parents. "What's going on? Miss Kelly says you have maggots in your ear?"

"Yes," I said.

"Um. No, that's ridiculous," he said firmly. "You have lice. One of the girls had a problem with lice just a few days ago."

Presumably the one who still had hair, I thought. But then remembered it didn't matter. He was probably lying for my parents' benefit.

"Oh, lice!" my dad said. "It's been a long time since I've heard anyone talk about lice." I was sure there was a regulation against them in Park Ridge.

"I guess we've over-reacted," my mom agreed.

"Well, we need to get on the road," my dad said. "And Jake needs a shampoo and maybe a haircut."

"Let's go into the exam room. I've got a lice comb in there," Dr. Harry said.

My parents watched as we walked into the exam room. As soon as the door was shut, I said, "It's not lice."

"Of course, not. Get up on the table while I find tweezers."

He opened and closed a few drawers, found the tweezers, and set a bottle of rubbing alcohol and a small plastic bottle with a nozzle like a bent straw on the counter. Then he filled the bottle with a mixture of water and rubbing alcohol.

"Lay on your side so I can get to your ear," he said.

I did as I was told. Dr. Harry set a little metal tray on the exam table beside me. Then he squirted the water mixture into my ear. It felt like an ice pick going in. To get to my ear, he needed to be close to me. He had an old man smell of booze and stale sweat.

"This is why I'm not willing to continue the study, Jake. Do you understand now?"

"I'm getting better. That's what you told Dr. Callabray."

He stopped for a moment, not liking that I knew things. He used a piece of gauze to soak up the fluid he'd dumped in my ear. And with it some of the maggots.

"That was a private conversation, Jake."

"You lied. I'm not getting better."

"No. You're not."

"But I might. If you told Dr. Callabray the truth."

He ignored that. "You need to stop going outside." Then he took the tweezers and began pulling maggots out of my ear one by one. It was tedious. Each time he pulled one out, I shivered. It tickled in the most disgusting way.

"Couldn't you just get me some bug repellent?"

"I'm not sure that would work. Flies are attracted by the smell of decay."

"What about Goth?"

"He can go out as much as he wants."

"No, I mean he's sick. He's getting sicker. You need to give him Property Five."

"I'm not continuing the study. It wouldn't be ethical."

Ethical? That was a weird word for him to use. The things in the double-wide, the frog, the rats, the little girl, none of that seemed ethical.

"He's going to die soon," I said.

"Yes. He is."

"You brought him here for me. So neither of us would be alone. You can't let him die."

"It's become more complicated."

"I'm rotting. I get it. But I'm conscious. Isn't there hope as long as I remain conscious?"

"Yes, of course, there is," Dr. Harry said. I wished he'd said in a more convincing tone. "Hold still."

He rinsed my ear out again.

"If there's hope for me, there's hope for others."

Dr. Harry didn't reply.

forty-six

When I got back to the ward after Dr. Harry had scraped out my ear and packed it with cotton, I went immediately to the bathroom. Positioning myself in front of the mirror, I pulled off the bandage and yanked out the cotton. I hadn't realized it before, but I wasn't hearing so well out of that ear. I mean, I probably didn't realize because I was still hearing all sorts of things I shouldn't hear with my other ear. I got all the cotton out and then...

I had to do it. I had to know. I slipped my finger into my ear. What I found made me shiver. Where my ear canal had been was a sort of cavern, ragged and rough around the edges, scooped out, hollow and already itching. I pulled my finger out and promised myself I'd never stick it back in again. I packed the cotton back into my ear and put the bandage back on. The tape had lost some of its adhesion, but after a few tries I got it to stick.

Stopping what I was doing, I just stared at myself. My dad was right. I was a little green, my lips were bluish and waxy. My skin was waxy too, like I was something out of a wax museum. I'd obviously lost weight, and deep caverns were below my cheeks. The only bright spot was my hair. It was still growing and didn't look as patchy as it used to.

Just then, Goth came into the bathroom. I looked at him sheepishly and said, "I had maggots in my ear. Dr. Harry got them out."

"Good."

"I can't go outside."

"Sunlight is over-rated." He leaned against the wall, looking cool, casual. It didn't occur to me he might be doing it because he could barely stand up. But that was probably the reason.

"I'm gross," I said.

"One thing CF has taught me is that life is gross."

For a weird second, I thought I was in a romantic comedy. He liked me even though I was gross. Actually, that was cool, very cool. My heart clenched, and I thought it might stop. What if Goth died? I doubted Dr. Harry was going to add anyone else to the study. I'd be alone. Well, except for the girls. But I didn't want the girls. And I didn't want Dr. Harry to find some other guy for the study later on after they got things fixed. I wanted Goth.

Spending time with him was the only time I felt truly alive anymore. Most of the time, I felt like an experiment on the verge of going wrong. A thing. A monster. But then, Goth would be there, and I was an almost normal teenager falling in love.

"There's something weird out in the trailer, isn't there?" he asked.

"No. It's just kind of moldy smelling."

"You went inside the other day. When we sat on the deck. You didn't want me to go in there. Is something in that weird refrigerator?"

"Just food."

"No. There's no food in there. If there was food, they'd be feeding us better than they are. What was it?"

I ignored the question and slipped my arm around his waist, tucking my head under his chin. I felt him rest his weight on me. "This is a stupid question, but my mom said I smell bad. I don't, do I?"

I braced myself for being told I smelled. Which, in all honestly would not have been the worst thing going on in my life. I felt him shrug. "My nose doesn't work that well. Symptom of my disease."

"Oh. Good to know."

"You're too cute to smell."

"I think that's the nicest lie anyone's ever told me." Of course that made me think about the lies I was telling Goth. Or rather the things I wasn't telling him. Which was kind of the same thing. I wasn't answering his questions about the refrigerated room. I wasn't telling him that I was in a constant state of dying—wow, it really was the un-sexiest phrase I'd ever heard.

"There's something bad happening to you, isn't there?" Goth asked quietly. "And it has something to do with whatever is in the refrigerator."

I was quiet, listening to him wheeze. I didn't know what to say. Telling him was just a bad idea. But I didn't want to lie to him, couldn't even think up a lie good enough that he'd believe it.

Finally, he said, "It's okay. You'll tell me when you're ready."

"If you could live forever, would you?" I asked.

Instantly, he said, "Yes, of course."

"You don't want to think about it?"

"Anyone who answers that question with a no is lying to you."

"But what if there are complications?"

"Life always has complications. Mortality being kind of a big one."

I should tell him. I should tell him everything.

"Goth. There's stuff we should talk about."

But I didn't tell him. I didn't say anything because I didn't even know where to start. Should I start by saying that Property Five didn't work? Except it did kind of work. I should say that Property Five kind of works. But then he'd think I was telling him he was going to get it soon. That we were working out the bugs. Literally.

Maybe I should start with the idea that I was dead. Although I shouldn't say it like that. I really needed to figure out a way to talk about what I was.

What was I? That stopped me. I'd just been figuring out who I was and where I fit in. But now I didn't fit in anywhere. It wasn't like I was going to get out of the Institute someday and go to college and join the Undead Gay Student Union. I wasn't going to be a proud Zombie-American. As far as I knew I was alone. Completely, utterly alone. Well, except for various body parts buried out back and a non-functional, partially decayed little girl. And maybe someday, Goth.

"Hey. You're not...talking."

"The bad thing that's happening to me. I can't die. But I'm not exactly alive either. I'm caught. In between."

forty-seven

Tuesday morning the girls left.

About an hour after Nurse Kelly finished with the basics, she led the girls out of the building one by one to a waiting minivan that said TJ's Medical Transport on the side. I guess that was who you called when you didn't exactly need an ambulance. As I watched through the window, I worried they were going to come and take Goth next. I was relieved when the van drove off.

"I guess it's just you and me now," Goth said, panting. His face a little red. Nurse Kelly wouldn't tell us how high his fever was, but the look on her face said it was pretty high.

We were both tired and fell back to sleep after that. We'd been up half the night, tented under Goth's blanket. I'd told him everything. All about the visions and Dr. Harry's boyfriends and the frog and the little girl and the terrible old men buried in pieces out in the yard. I told him about my mom, too. How she'd never really asked if I wanted to come to the Institute, never really told me what Dr. Harry was studying even. That she knew what was happening to me all along.

"Are you going to be able to forgive her?"

"She's my mom. I kind of have to."

Goth looked thoughtful for a moment, which made me ask, "I know it all sounds crazy but— You believe me don't you?"

"I do. I mean I wouldn't except that you're making sense out of things that didn't make sense. It didn't make sense that we were all sick in different ways. It didn't make sense that Dr. Harry just let Edmond die. And it didn't make sense that Dr. Harry is canceling everything. But now it kind of does."

"And now that you know everything, do you still, you know, want to be like me?"

"I don't want to die."

"You're not going to die. I won't let you."

And as soon as I said that, I forgave my mom. I had to. I was starting to understand how she felt.

A car door slamming woke me up, and I saw the black Heartwell van sitting in front of the Institute. It pulled away and was gone. I was still kind of sleep-drunk and wondered if I'd really seen it. I had, though. I'd seen it. Goth was asleep in the bed next to me. The Heartwell van had come to pick something up and it wasn't me or Goth—we were right there —and it wasn't any of the girls because they were already gone. So who was it?

Dr. Harry was closing down the study. But why would he do that? Were things really that bad with me? Something popped into my head. I left the ward, hurried through the solarium and out the back door. I dashed across the yard to the double-wide and then circled around the back so I could climb up onto the deck. The sliding glass door in the back was locked. I pulled at it a few times and gave up. I checked the window over the kitchen sink. Also locked. The door into the utility room. Locked. The window in the utility room. Open. But very, very small.

I took off my bathrobe and dumped it in a pile on the deck. Then I squeezed myself through the very small window. It was just above the washing machine so it wasn't too difficult to pull myself in. I had to twist my hips to get them through the window. Moments later, I was crawling off the washing machine.

I stepped out into the hallway and turned toward the refrigerated room. For some reason, Dr. Harry hadn't put a new lock on the door. That was odd. Did he really think that just locking up the trailer would keep the things inside from getting out?

Opening the door to the room, I felt a burst of chilled air wrap around me. I stepped inside and immediately saw why Dr. Harry hadn't bothered with a new lock. The walk-in was empty. The girl, the mice, the past experiments, they were all gone.

forty-eight

"We have to find a way out of here," Goth whispered to me after the Heartwell mortuary took the experiments away.

"When my mom comes back, we'll leave with her," I whispered.

"But she's not coming until Friday. Can we wait that long?"

He had a point. Dr. Harry seemed to be moving quickly. The girls were gone. The experiments were gone. If he was shutting things down, the only two details left were me and Goth. "I should call her."

I went out to the nurses' desk and asked Nurse Kelly if I could use the phone.

"Sure," she said without thinking. "Go ahead."

I slid the phone toward me and dialed. Nurse Kelly was filling out some kind of form. It took a moment before I realized I'd never gotten a dial tone. "Um, I don't think the phone is working."

"Oh, yeah, that's right. They turned it off."

"Why did they turn the phone off?"

"Um, I don't know." That was an obvious lie. She knew, she just wasn't saying. "Maybe it'll be back on tomorrow."

I went back into the ward and sat on the edge of my bed. Goth was almost through his Faulkner book. "They turned the phone off so I couldn't call my mom."

"What? They don't want you to call your mom?"

"No, I mean, they turned off the landline. I *couldn't* call my mom."

"Why would they do that?"

"I think because they're shutting the place down."

"Yeah, but we're still here."

Goth opened the drawer of his nightstand. He pulled out his phone and clicked it on. Handing it to me, he said, "It's half-charged. Walk out to the edge of the property until you get a signal."

I took the phone. "Do you want to come with me?"

"I think I over did it last night," he said with a devilish smile and a hacking cough.

I couldn't help but smile back. Slipping the phone into my pocket, I walked out of the ward and then down the hall to the solarium. I wished I had something to put into my ears. I didn't want the flies to get at me again. This is just going to take five minutes, I told myself. I just need to get my mom on the phone and see if she can come sooner.

I reached out to open the door to the outside and found that it was locked. Stupidly, I shook the door. I knew that wouldn't help, so I don't know why I did it. I took a step back. It had been open just a half an hour before. Should I try to break through the door? It was kind of flimsy. Was that really where I was? Breaking through doors?

"Jake? What are you doing?" Dr. Harry said behind me.

I spun around. "Why is the door locked?"

"Because you shouldn't be going outside. I don't want to have to pull maggots out of your ear again."

"Why did you turn the landline off? I need to call my mom."

"There's no need to worry. We've let your family know that you're incommunicado for the time being. You'll see your mother on Friday."

"Is there a way I can talk to her now? Can you turn off the jammer so I can call her?"

"Jammer? What are you talking about, Jake?"

"You have a jammer so no one can make calls."

"That's ridiculous. Cell coverage in this area is terrible. On top of that, something about the way these old buildings were made interferes with any signal that does get through."

"I need to call my mom. Can you help me do that?"

"But I just said you don't need to call her. She'll be here on Friday."

I didn't know what to say. He was being really reasonable, but it was so weird and so wrong at the same time. I didn't know what else to say but "Okay, sure, I'll just go back to the ward."

I tried to ease around him, but he grabbed me by the arm. "I'm sorry. I'm sorry you can't talk to your mother." It sounded like he was apologizing for a lot more than that.

Pulling my arm back, I mumbled "Thanks," and hurried back to the ward. When I got there, I gave Goth his phone and told him about the locked door and running into Dr. Harry.

"What are we going to do?" he asked.

We had to do something. We couldn't wait until Friday. I needed my mom to come get us now. But how could I reach her?

forty-nine

While I tried to figure out what to do next, Goth got sicker. He was on oxygen all the time. Every so often, he hacked some blood into a handkerchief. It was terrible to watch. Of course, it was probably the reason he was still there. He was *too* sick. There probably weren't any hospitals nearby that could handle transporting him. Even in an ambulance with lights flashing, breaking the speed limit, he might not make it. And that might attract attention to the Institute.

I sat next to the bed holding his hand most of the afternoon. I didn't know what to do. I couldn't reach my mom and wasn't even sure if it mattered anymore. Goth needed Property Five, or he wasn't going to make it. Somehow, I had to get my hands on it. I knew where it was. But the door was locked. I could project myself into the room but I couldn't unlock the cabinet. Couldn't pick up the vial of Property Five. Couldn't bring it downstairs.

"I'm not going to make it," Goth whispered. "Thank you, though."

"You're going to be okay. I'll figure something out."

"It was worth coming here just to meet you. Just to cross a few things off my bucket list."

"No, don't give up. Do you hear me? I'm going to find a way to get you Property Five. And then, on Friday my mom will come, and we'll go to Dr. Callabray, and he'll take care of us."

He smiled at me weakly.

"Goth, tell me you won't give up."

"Bae, talking hurts."

"Promise me you won't give up. Just nod."

He nodded.

I relaxed a little. But only a little. I needed to get into the lab. I needed to find the key. I wondered for a moment if there was a key in the reception desk. It would be easy enough to wait until Nurse Kelly went to the bathroom and get it then. But, I really didn't think Dr. Harry trusted any of the nurses enough to leave the key—

Wait, Miss Haggerty had a key. Did that mean there were keys in the desk? Or did it just mean Miss Haggerty had one? From where I sat, I could see Nurse Kelly's back. She wore teddy bear scrubs. A super-sized cola sat on the desk. She and Goth had had Mickey D's again for lunch, though Goth had barely touched his. Too weak to eat.

With just Goth and me there, Nurse Kelly didn't have much to do. She was reading a bestseller from the supermarket and sipping her pop every few minutes. It was just a matter of time before she had to go to the bathroom. Almost forty minutes later, she got up from the desk and walked to the back of the building to use the bathroom attached to the girl's ward.

I was at the desk almost immediately. I opened the center drawer and found nothing. Oh my God, did she have the keys in her pocket? It flashed in my mind that I might have to try and mug Nurse Kelly but then I saw the keys sitting in a pink coffee cup that said, DON'T MESS WITH ME I GET PAID TO STICK PEOPLE WITH SHARP OBJECTS. I snatched them up.

Heart pounding in my ears. I went up the stairs to the second floor. Trying not to catch glass Jesus's eye at the landing, I climbed up, up, until I was in the hallway. I went right to the laboratory door. I flipped through the key ring, trying to decide which key to start with. The first few didn't work. Then, I found the one that did. I was in the laboratory.

The first thing I noticed was boxes on all the counters. Dr. Harry was leaving, too. He wasn't just sending the subjects away, he was shutting everything down. I searched for the glass cabinet to make sure the Property Five was still there. It was.

I hurried to the filing cabinet where I'd seen Miss Haggerty get the key to the glass cabinet. The drawer was empty. I ran my hand around the bottom of the metal drawer until I found the key. Then, I hurried back to the glass cabinet and the padlock. Lifting the padlock, I slipped the key in and turned. The lock came off and I opened the cabinet.

Before I could reach in and take out the Property Five, I felt a sting on the back of my neck, like a bee or a fly. I reached back to swat the fly away and grabbed Dr. Harry by the hand. I spun around to look at him, my knees already getting rubbery, his face sliding around—

fifty

My first thought when I woke up was that I was back in Niles in my own bed again. It even crossed my mind that everything had been a dream, and I'd never gone to The Godwin Institute; that my mom and I had never driven to Michigan at all. But my neck was stiff and when I moved my head to try to ease the discomfort, my nose scraped across thin, crinkly plastic.

When I opened my eyes, I saw nothing but black. I reminded myself to breathe and inhaled the stuffy, acrid smell of newly minted plastic. I raised my hands to my face and along the way found a zipper running up and down from my hips to my forehead, as though bisecting me.

I was in a body bag.

The zipper pull, of course, was on the outside of the bag. It took me a minute or so to work my index finger through the zipper so that I could force it down. It wasn't easy, getting the right angle. Of course, the bag was not designed to be opened from the inside. Once I got the zipper open about six inches, I was able to slip my hand through and pull it down to around my hips. I sat up. Or rather, I tried to sit up. When I did, I brushed my head against what felt like heavy cardboard.

I lay back down and felt around. Yes, it was cardboard. I was in a bag, inside a box. I shook my head from side to side for a moment trying to decide whether I was dreaming. It didn't make sense, so it had to be a dream. Except it didn't feel like a dream at all.

I pushed on the cardboard above my head. Something held it down. I pushed harder, raising my knees and pushing with them. The box had a lid, but the lid did not want to come off. And then, the cardboard over my face began to rip. Outside the box, it was only a tiny bit brighter than the complete dark inside. I kept pulling at the rip until it was a slash, a gash, a hole, a flap. Once I'd made the opening big enough, I put both of my arms through it and raised myself to a sitting position.

The room was dark, but my eyes adjusted, and I could make most of it out. The walls were covered in large tiles, possibly green. I couldn't be sure. I'd been lying on some kind of conveyor belt. In the darkness in front of me, I could see the gaping maw of an oven. It was cold. Edges scarred by flames. I could see part of a metal door that would close after I was pushed inside.

I sat on the conveyor collecting myself, breathing, because it was good for me and it felt good. I tried to decide if my heart was beating. I checked my pulse. If it was there, it was too faint for me to find. I began coughing, hoping that would compress my heart, then I started to pound on my chest. I'd pound and wait, pound and wait. Finally, I felt my heart flip and push rhythmically against my rib cage.

It was night. Somehow Dr. Harry had gotten me there, put me into a body bag, then inside this cardboard coffin and left me to be cremated first thing in the morning. Slowly, I pieced together how that must have happened. The last thing I remembered was being in the lab. I must have passed out as soon as whatever he gave me hit my bloodstream.

Clumsily, I struggled to climb out of the bag and the collapsing coffin, landing on the concrete floor before I managed to wiggle my way out of both. The bag and the coffin came with me, and I lay on the floor, kicking my way out of them. I was still in my pajamas, but barefoot. The floor felt warm though, but that only meant it was warmer than I was. I got onto my feet. The room I was in felt like a garage, no windows, a door that rolled up—for deliveries, I guessed. Some light slipped through chips in the blackout windows in the garage door. The moon was out, and it might have been full, I couldn't remember.

Stumbling to the door, I felt around for a light switch but instead found the button that opened the door. With a loud jolt, the door began to roll up. When it reached the top, I went out into the parking lot of the funeral home. It was strangely bright. Looking up at the sky I found I was right. The moon was nearly full. The sky was cloudless but windy. Heavy, constant, howling wind.

I walked around to the front of the funeral home and saw a sign that read, HEARTWELL'S. Yeah, I wasn't surprised. To my left and right was a small town, running only a few blocks in each direction: a couple of restaurants, a gas station, a few clothing stores, a movie theater, a post office. Pretty much like my mom had said.

Everything was closed. It must have been two, three in the morning. At the end of the street, a yellow caution light swung in the wind over the empty intersection. I didn't know the name of the street in front of me or even the name of the town.

Despite the wind, flies began to swarm me. I waved my hands a few times, but I couldn't be bothered. I had to get back to The Godwin Institute. Was the B&B my mother stayed in nearby? Where was it? What had she said about the area? There were no chain stores in town. I remembered that. I had no idea whether to walk left or right. The Institute could be in either direction, or even behind me. No, no, it wasn't behind me. I could see a sign that said MARINA half a block away with an arrow pointing in the direction I was facing. The lake was in front of me. That meant the Institute was either to the left or right.

I had to figure out which direction. I had to get back there. I had to get back to Goth. I didn't think Dr. Harry would do anything to him except send him somewhere he was sure to die, but I hadn't thought Dr. Harry would send me to a funeral home to be incinerated. And that made me wonder, why had I woken up? Had he not given me enough medicine? Was that why my body felt thick? And my mind—

Wait. A car was coming, light from its headlights bounced against the small businesses. I thought to step out into the street to stop them and ask them to bring me back to the Institute. But what story would I tell? I was a barefoot, pale-faced young man in pajamas wandering out of a funeral home in the middle of the night with a swarm of flies around him. If I was lucky and stopped a Good Samaritan, I'd be taken to a hospital. The police might be called. I didn't want that. I stepped back into the Heartwell's doorway. The car sped by.

Think. How could I figure out which direction to go in? The lake was north. The Institute faced the lake. When we arrived, the lake had been to my left when I got out of the car. I didn't remember coming through this town. Did that mean the town was east of the Godwin Institute and I should turn west?. Was that right? I had no idea. But I knew I couldn't stand in front of a funeral home until morning. I had to at least try to get back. I began walking west.

As I lumbered down the street, my legs still wooden from whatever drug I was given, the businesses quickly thinned and I passed clapboard houses that were, like, a hundred years old. Some of them had businesses in the front: a lawyer, a yarn shop, a store that sold spices. I pushed on.

Another car came toward me. I ignored it, but the car slowed. Why would someone do that? Well, it *was* a small town. People knew each other, and I was in my pajamas. I might be in trouble. I was in trouble.

As the car got closer, I saw it was one of those cars that's half SUV and half mini-station wagon. A woman about my mother's age was driving. She slowed almost to a stop. An empty baby seat was in the back. A mom coming home after a free night with a girlfriend or two. She was almost stopped, leaning over the passenger seat to get a look at me. I waved her on. Concern flashed across her face, then, as she got a good look at me, fear. The car suddenly jerked forward and sped down the street.

I hoped that wouldn't happen too many more times. I could imagine the story the woman was going to tell her husband, that she'd almost stopped for a young man in pajamas, but when she slowed, she saw that he was...horrible, a monster, staggering as though not completely alive. Her husband would laugh and make a joke about his favorite zombie movie. Or maybe she'd insist she saw a ghost, and her husband would tease her about that. And then lecture her about having too many drinks before driving.

How far was I going to have to walk? My mom drove most of the times she had come to see me, but she'd said that there was a trail she was going to walk. Had she done that? Had she walked to come see me? Even if she'd only thought about it, I couldn't be too far from the Institute. I pushed on.

At the very end of the town, I found another caution light swinging in the wind. There was one at each end of town. It wasn't even a big enough place for an actual stoplight. At this end of town, the light hung over a T-intersection connecting with what looked like a major route. I was looking for a route number, not that it would have made any sense to me, but it would make me feel better. A route number meant the road was connected to the rest of the world, but all I could see was a street sign, Duck Pond Road.

But then, almost at the same time, I saw the sign for the Meehawnee Trail. The entrance to the trail was half a block up Duck Pond Road. The sidewalk ended. I was walking on gravel and sand. It should have hurt my feet, but it didn't. I glanced behind me and saw my footprints in the sandy gravel; I was leaving drag marks. I reminded myself to pick up my feet.

What had I been given? And how much? Was it enough to kill me if I'd still been alive? I pushed the thought from my mind. I couldn't think about that. I had to get back to the Institute before Dr. Harry sent Goth away.

The trail was paved, about as wide as a truck. I was barely a hundred feet in, and everything around me was wild. The wind rustled the leaves rhythmically. Tiny hands clapping. Fifty feet from the trail, there was a line of birch trees and poplars and some kind of evergreen. The trail was thick with them, but they seemed to have a terrible habit of dying. In amongst the living, growing trees were dozens that had died. They stood there, naked, craggy, beaten gray by the weather. Nearly glowing in the moonlight. The dead among the living.

I walked. Pulling myself forward. Step by step. Willing my feet to rise, one after the other. The trail seemed to lift, running along some kind of berm, with sitting water on either side of me. For a moment, that didn't make sense. But then I thought about how close we were to the lake. These were wetlands. The land rose where I could see trees, and where it sank there was water that barely seemed to move. And cattails. Rows of cattails.

The stars were out, the sky cloudless. The moon full and bright. Something about it so magical, majestic. I never saw the sky like this. We were too near Chicago to see stars. Somehow it gave me a feeling of peace, even in the midst of the mess that was now my life. As long as there were stars, it would be all right.

And then I saw the crows.

There were seven or eight of them flying above me. As I walked, they seemed to stay with me. Waiting. I was afraid they'd dip down and attack me at first, but I didn't think crows were like that. Hawks were like that.

And eagles. Crows waited until something was dead. They lived off road-kill and whatever dead things ended up in the woods. For a moment, I felt safer. And then I remembered I wasn't all that different from roadkill. I just moved a lot more.

How would I know when to leave the path? How would I find the Institute? I tried to remember if I'd seen any landmarks when I was out in the back. I couldn't remember any, though. It would be to my right, I knew that. The lake was to my right. Maybe I was wrong, though, maybe I should have stayed on the main road. That would have brought me to the Institute eventually. Now I was—

Up in front of me, I saw a flash. A tiny flame. A lighter. All at once, gray figures separated themselves from the silhouetted shrubs and trees. Four people were standing on or near the trail. One of them was smoking a cigarette. Well, not a cigarette, I realized as he passed it to the person next to him.

"Good stuff," I heard him say, though I wasn't close to them.

"My sister caught me when I was climbing out the window," the girl said. One of them was a girl. Maybe two of them were. I couldn't tell.

"No shit."

"Is she going to tell on you?"

"Naw. She was climbing in the window. That's how she caught me."

"Oh man. You're frigging kidding me."

"I wish I could tell on her, though. Her boyfriend is the biggest asshole I've ever met."

Of course it was hard to imagine she'd met many big assholes in her time. She was still sneaking out of her parents' house. She couldn't be too old. I decided avoiding them was a good idea. The image I'd create stepping out of the dark would likely cause them to have all sorts of wrong ideas. Or maybe not so wrong.

I stepped off the trail. Trying to avoid the wet places, I picked my way through the brush in the dim light. The feeling in my feet was beginning to come back, and I started to feel the twigs and stones I stepped on. I tried to make a wide arc around the teenagers who were still talking.

"So, what *is* that place?" a boy asked. "My mom said they used to keep the retards there."

"Nooooo," the girl replied, completely exasperated. "It was a Catholic boys' school. My father went there."

We were close to the Institute. That had to be what they were talking about. Could it be seen from the trail? It was possible. I hadn't spent enough time in the back to know what could be seen through the stand of trees.

"So my mom was right. It *was* a place for retards."

"There's nothing wrong with my dad and stop saying that word. It's not nice."

Suddenly, in the muck, I stepped on a thin dry branch that broke with a loud snap. The snap was immediately followed by one of the girls screaming.

"Oh my God, something's out there."

I froze. I wanted to run, but I couldn't afford to make any more noise. I didn't want them coming after me.

"It's just a deer," a boy said.

"What if it isn't a deer? What if it's someone, someone horrible?"

"Then the monster will jump out and eat us. You've seen too many horror movies."

"Most horror movies are based on real life, jackass."

"Yeah, like *Human Centipede* is totally based on real shit." That was another of the boys. He sounded drunker than the first one.

"You're just freaked because you're from the city," the first boy said. "People who come up from the city are always a little afraid. Like they think cannibals are going to jump out of every bush."

"Cannibal movies are real," asserted the girl. "*Texas Chainsaw Massacre* really happened."

"Which time? There's like a dozen versions of that..."

I took a chance and stumbled through a few more steps. Stepping on another branch resulted in another scream. This time though, I decided to take a chance and start running. The noise would terrify them. There was a fifty-fifty chance they'd run in the other direction.

For what seemed like a really long time, I didn't know if they'd come after me. I was making so much noise myself thudding through the swampy thicket that I had no idea if someone was behind me.

I might have heard a whisper of one of them saying, "We have to get out of here" but I couldn't be sure.

Finally, I worked my way back to the path, finding myself in front of a wooden bridge made of graying planks stretching across a rushing stream.

I pulled myself across the bridge, listening for the teenagers. They were silent. They must have gone in the other direction since I couldn't hear them.

It wasn't much longer when I saw a faint light through the trees. It had to be the Institute. The light was coming from the nurses' station at the front of the building. I was seeing it through the windows in the solarium. As I got directly behind the Institute, the light disappeared. It must have been blocked out by the double-wide. Yes, I'd found it.

Now what? I wasn't sure. My thoughts were half-formed. Almost pre-verbal. Primal. I had to get in. That was all I knew. I had to get inside.

I stepped off the trail, glancing down at my feet as I did. They were filthy. My pajamas were ripped, and I had cuts that oozed but didn't bleed. I was going to have to get through the trees and brush between the trail and the Institute. I had no choice.

I picked my way through. More dirt, more scrapes, but in just a couple of minutes, I was in back of the Institute. I could clearly see the double-wide, the garden beds, the prairie. I kept pushing forward. I might have been able to sneak in through the solarium, but I walked around to the front of the building instead. I wasn't thinking deception. I was thinking confrontation.

fifty-one

I pushed open the front door. Ray sat at the front desk with a quizzical look on his face, a newspaper open in front of him. He was trying to work a crossword puzzle but not doing well, I could see that half of it was painted over with Wite-Out. He jumped up when he heard the door, his snakish face contorting when he saw me. I wasn't sure if he was freaked by the way I looked—flies, mud, blood—or by the simple fact that I was up and moving around.

"No, no, you're—"

"I'm what? Inside a body bag waiting to be cremated in the morning?"

"Dr. Harry! Dr. Harry! Come down here!"

He fumbled with the phone for a moment. It didn't work, of course. He was about to get up from the desk when I picked up the pen he'd been using and drove it through the back of his hand. "Jesus Christ! Oh my God!"

While he was screaming, I picked up a pencil from a small leather cup that held about a dozen pens and pencils and drove it into his chest. I must have hit something vital because he stopped yelling and plunked down into the desk chair. A bloody bubble popped up onto his lip. I wasn't sure if I'd killed him, but it didn't matter. I was pretty sure he wouldn't be bothering me.

I snatched the keys out of the pink cup with the funky saying about stabbing people. Funny, huh? Glancing into the ward, I saw Goth laid out in bed, oxygen pumping. But he wasn't moving. That sealed my resolve. I lumbered up the stairs slowly. Watching Jesus in the stained-glass window, caught forever in his ascent to heaven. I wondered why it wasn't blasphemy to show Jesus trapped between heaven and earth. Never entering heaven. Never returning to earth. Caught between life and death, just like me.

I was stepping onto the landing in front of the window when Dr. Harry came running down the stairs.

"How did you get here?"

I kept climbing, up, up, up. "You tried to destroy me."

"Jake, you have to see reason," he said, following me. "There was always the possibility the experiment might fail. You have to have known that."

Pushing by him, I reached the second floor and aimed myself toward the lab. He followed me.

"Can't you see what I did was a kindness?"

I stood in front of the lab and flipped through the key ring to find the key.

"Your life will just keep getting worse and worse. You'll continue to decay. You'll never be able to leave here. Never be able to go back to your life."

"That's not what Dr. Callabray thinks. He wants to move forward. He wants to save me."

The door opened, and I was in the lab. I lurched over to the filing cabinet and got the key to the glass cabinet.

"Callabray just wants to make money. He doesn't care about you."

"You care so much about me you wanted to incinerate me."

I slipped the key into the padlock. Dr. Harry tried to stop me, and I slapped his hands away. Reaching inside I grabbed a vial of Property Five and a syringe and needle wrapped in plastic.

"Jake, I thought, I hoped if I did that, you might have some peace."

"These are my choices. Not yours. Mine!"

I aimed myself out of the lab into the hallway. I had to get downstairs to Goth. I had to give him Property Five.

"I'm sorry, but I don't think it is your choice," Dr. Harry said, following me. "I'm the one responsible. I'm the one who gave you Property Five. The flies buzzing around your head are my fault. The pallor of your skin. The cuts and scrapes that will never heal. The stench that follows you. All my responsibility."

"I am not a thing. I am a person. I get to decide."

"No. You don't."

I was halfway down the stairs when he pushed me, trying to knock me down the stairs to the landing. Instead, I fell against the wall and caught the railing. Righting myself, I reached up and grabbed him by the collar, pulling him down the stairs. He wasn't expecting it. He lost his footing. He seemed to recover for a moment, but it was gone quickly, and he seemed to run, tripping, picking up speed and then turning to look at me, fell backward into the stained-glass window.

He hit it with a hard thud. The window bent. The lead strips looked like they might hold it together, but pieces began to pop out. Christ's foot, a bit of his robe, the ground beneath the savior.

Dr. Harry seemed to relax. He must have thought he'd be able to untangle himself from the window when a ray of light emanating from Christ's halo loosened itself and fell into Dr. Harry's neck just between his collar and his beard. Nothing happened. A tiny bit of blood rose to the surface around the shard of glass.

I walked down the stairs and stood in front of him. Gingerly, he felt around his neck. He'd severed a major artery and the only reason he wasn't spurting blood everywhere was that the glass kept that from happening.

I reached out to pull the glass from his neck.

"Please. Please don't."

"You're going to die," I told him. "You might as well get it over with."

His eyes were wild. "No, no, I can't. Give me Property Five. Then I can help you. I'll help you give it to Goliath."

"After everything you did, everything you said, you want me to save you?"

"You need me, Jake. Please. I want to live."

"So do I," I said as I pulled the shard of glass out of his neck.

fifty-two

I wanted to live. Ironic, I know. I'd wanted to die and then I did. Now that I was dead, I wanted to live. I guess what they say is true. The grass is always greener. Of course, it would be nice if staying alive were as easy as growing grass.

When I went into the ward, I saw Goth in his bed, pale and struggling to breathe. I hurried over as best I could.

"I have it. Just hold on a second."

"They stopped giving me antibiotics. Dr. Harry is letting me die. He called it benign neglect."

"Dr. Harry is dead."

"How—"

"I'll tell you later" I said, setting the vial of Property Five on the nightstand. I opened the plastic seal on the needle kit and put the hypodermic together. Then I stuck the needle into the vial and turned the whole thing upside down, pulling back the plunger and filling the syringe with Property Five. Then, I looked for bubbles, flicking it with my finger to make one spring to the top. I'd seen nurses do that. I wasn't entirely sure why, but I thought the bubbles were a problem. I squirted a little bit of Property Five out and then I was ready.

I turned back to Goth. "I'm not sure if I can do this."

"Heroin addicts do it. I think you can." His breath was thick, raspy.

"Heroin addicts have had a lot more practice than I've had."

But I had no choice. He wanted me to do it. Too late I realized I had no disinfectant. No cotton swab. I let the syringe hover over Goth's arm but didn't try to find a vein. Could I do this? Could I really do this?

His arm was bruised from all the needle sticks he'd had in the past few weeks. And then there were the scars. Scars from years of being stuck.

"There's a vein. Right here," he said. "Near the surface." He pointed to a particular spot well below his elbow. "I always tell the nurse. It usually works out. Just slap my arm."

He didn't wait for me to do it, though. He did it himself. Two times. Three times. The vein popped to the surface. I could see it.

"You're sure. You're sure you want to do this?"

"Yes. I want this," he said, nearly out of breath. "Hurry."

I took hold of his arm and aimed the needle at his vein. I concentrated on not going too deep but going deep enough. Sliding in, what, an eighth of an inch? A sixteenth? I knew I was supposed to do something, like pull the plunger back and see if blood came into the syringe. But I didn't. I just pressed the plunger down until all of the fluid had gone into Goth. All of the Property Five. It looked like I did it right. Nothing bad happened, anyway.

Goth slipped an arm around my neck and pulled me down to him.

"What happens next?"

"I think you're going to die."

"What? No. I'm going to—"

"You die and then you live. Like I did."

He looked confused. But it didn't matter. He didn't have to understand what was happening for this to work. I slipped my arms around him as his breathing became more labored. His lips blue. His skin pale.

"What if it doesn't work?" Goth's eyes searched mine.

"Don't be afraid," I told him.

His eyes rolled back, and he took a few strangled breaths.

When he died, I laid him back on the bed and went to the exam room. I opened the cupboard where Dr. Harry kept the portable defibrillator I'd become so damn familiar with. I brought the defibrillator into the ward, spread gel onto the paddles, opened Goth's pajamas and put the paddles onto his chest. Then I pressed the button on the right-hand paddle.

Nothing happened.

I wondered if I should up the amount of electricity, but I wasn't even sure how to do that. I decided to try just shocking him again. His chest bounced a bit this time. I placed my hand on his chest to see if I could feel his heart beating. As I did, he opened his eyes. He smiled at me and mumbled, "I'm here."

I caressed his cheek with one hand. He was already cooling. That made me happier than I'd been in a very long time.

I wasn't alone. There was someone like me.

We were two.

also by marshall thornton

IN THE BOYSTOWN MYSTERIES

The Boystown Prequels
(Little Boy Dead & Little Boy Afraid)
Boystown: Three Nick Nowak Mysteries
Boystown 2: Three More Nick Nowak Mysteries
Boystown 3: Two Nick Nowak Novellas
Boystown 4: A Time for Secrets
Boystown 5: Murder Book
Boystown 6: From the Ashes
Boystown 7: Bloodlines
Boystown 8: The Lies That Bind
Boystown 9: Lucky Days
Boystown 10: Gifts Given
Boystown 11: Heart's Desire
Boystown 12: Broken Cord
Boystown 13: Fade Out

IN THE PINX VIDEO MYSTERIES

Night Drop
Hidden Treasures
Late Fees
Rewind
Cash Out
Help Wanted
Kapowie!

IN THE WYANDOT COUNTY MYSTERIES

The Less Than Spectacular Times of Henry Milch

A Fabulously Unfabulous Summer for Henry Milch

The Fall and Rise of Henry Milch

IN THE DOM REILLY MYSTERIES

Year of the Rat

A Mean Season

The Happy Month

OTHER BOOKS

The Perils of Praline

Desert Run

Full Release

The Ghost Slept Over

My Favorite Uncle

Femme

Praline Goes to Washington

Aunt Belle's Time Travel & Collectibles

Masc

Never Rest

Code Name: Liberty

Fathers of the Bride

Sentenced to Christmas

about the author

Marshall Thornton writes two popular mystery series, the *Boystown Mysteries* and the *Pinx Video Mysteries*. He has won the Lambda Award for Gay Mystery three times. His romantic comedy, *Femme* was also a 2016 Lambda finalist for Best Gay Romance, as was his romantic suspense novel, *Code Name: Liberty*. Other books include *My Favorite Uncle*, *The Ghost Slept Over* and *Masc,* the sequel to *Femme.* He is a member of Mystery Writers of America.